IN THE STREETZ 2

THE FALL

TRON HILL

URBAN AINT DEAD

URBAN AINT DEAD
P.O Box 448
Maybrook, NY 12543

Copyright © 2024 By Tron Hill

Cover Design: : P. Wise / The Wise Services

Edited By: Shawna Brim / Ladies Of Lit

URBAN AINT DEAD and coinciding logo(s) are registered properties.

Contact Publisher at www.urbanaintdead.com

Email: urbanaintdead@gmail.com

Print ISBN: 979-8-9906748-2-0

STAY UP TO DATE

To stay up to date on new releases, plus get information on contests,
sneak peaks and more,
Click the link below...
https://mailchi.mp/6d21003686d1/subscribe

CONTENTS

Soundtracks 7
Urban Aint Dead 9
Submissions 11

Prologue 13
Chapter 1 23
Chapter 2 31
Chapter 3 48
Chapter 4 57
Chapter 5 68
Chapter 6 79
Chapter 7 93
Chapter 8 98
Chapter 9 105
Chapter 10 124
Chapter 11 145
Chapter 12 161
Chapter 13 168

Review 179
Other Books By 181
Coming Soon 185
Books By 187
Stay Connected 189

<u>**Soundtracks**</u>

Scan the QR Code below to listen to the Soundtracks/Singles of some
of your favorite U.A.D titles:

Don't have Spotify or Apple Music?
No Sweat!
Visit your choice streaming platform and search URBAN AINT
DEAD.

Currently on lock serving a bid?
JPay, iHeartRadio, WHATEVER!
We got you covered.

Simply log into your facility's kiosk or tablet, go to music and search
URBAN AINT DEAD.

URBAN AINT DEAD

Like & Follow us on social media:
FB - URBAN AINT DEAD
IG: @urbanaintdead
Tik Tok - @urbanaintdead

<u>Submissions</u>

Submit the first three chapters of your completed manuscript to <u>urbanaintdead@gmail.com</u>, subject line: Your book's title. The manuscript must be in a .doc file and sent as an attachment. The document should be in Times New Roman, double-spaced, and in size 12 font. Also, provide your synopsis and full contact information. If sending multiple submissions, they must each be in a separate email. Have a story but no way to submit it electronically? You can still submit to URBAN AINT DEAD. Send in the first three chapters, written or typed, of your completed manuscript to:

URBAN AINT DEAD
P.O Box 448
Maybrook, NY 12543

DO NOT send original manuscript. Must be a duplicate.
Provide your synopsis and a cover letter containing your full contact information.
Thanks for considering URBAN AINT DEAD.

PROLOGUE

"**S**hhhiiit!" D-nice growled strongly through clenched gold teeth. He sat on the sofa, pants down to his ankles, legs spread eagle, while he masturbated to the porno playing on the sixty-four-inch flat screen TV. This was his usual routine whenever he was at the spot alone, which was a majority of the time.

Now, D-nice was the opposite of attractive face wise. Bumps had covered his face in puberty and had continued to dominate it into his adult years. When they would leave, they left hideous black marks which were no better than the bumps themselves.

However, that wasn't the reason he didn't have a girl. He always felt that having a girl, or what niggas liked to say, "they bitch", was something which added more complications to his way of life. It meant penetrating the boundaries of a thing he'd refused to socialize with. Love.

He had encountered the meaning of the word once in his teen years with the girl who stood as the monument of it. Mesha had been her name. D-nice would always remember the first time he saw his beautiful life, which resided in her.

Mesha and her family had just moved to the east side of Atlanta

"

from Detroit due to her brothers' involvement in gang affiliation, which put their entire family in danger.

When D-nice first caught sight of her, he knew he had to have her, but he was shy. He'd sit on his porch, waiting to be satisfied with the brief appearances she would make throughout any given day. Every time he saw her, his heart would beat against the inside walls of his chest. His pupils would become dilated as If he'd consumed some type of intoxicant. Existence would vanish, giving room for her very own realm, one in which he'd die to be in.

After a few months, he couldn't take it anymore. Could he have such a beautiful creation? He had to know because his obsession began to wear thin.

Finally, he'd stumbled across enough courage to at least become acquainted with her. If nothing more, he had to know her name. He had to hear her voice. One day, she'd come from the confinement of her home to retrieve the contents of her mailbox. D-nice saw the perfect opportunity to approach. She flipped through the envelopes, unaware of the visitor quickly coming up on her from behind.

"Hi," he spoke shyly, tapping her on her shoulder, causing her to spin around quickly to the touch.

"Hi," she responded a little uneasily at the boy who stood before her smiling stupidly.

"My name… My name…" Damn, he couldn't remember his own name. Everything began to spin faster and faster in his world to the point of him becoming lightheaded. D-nice tilted forward a bit then rocked backwards before the day turned to sudden blackness.

He couldn't remember what he was doing or where he was. Clouds were present everywhere. A dim light made it possible to distinguish them. He wondered if this was the first stages of death. Right then, he heard the angelic voice speak.

"Hey, hey, are you okay?" Then, the sun rays blazed over the head and shoulder of an angel.

Damn, it seemed as if he was in Heaven. There were clouds and the beautiful face. Then, he heard his grandmother shout, "Boy, get yo ass up! Ain't nothing wrong wit you."

After a minute, his eyes finally adjusted to the daylight's glow. He saw that beautiful face staring down at him, smiling. Lifting up a bit, he sat back on his elbows, giving a little shake to his head to focus. He glanced up at his grandma. "Granny, what happened?"

"Ion know, but I know you better get yo butt off this ground in them school clothes," she snapped with her hands on her hips as she pivoted around, heading back toward her house.

Helping him to his feet, the girl introduced herself. "My name Mesha."

Dang, he wanted to smile because she was touching him. "I'm… I mean, my name D-nice. What happened?" He didn't know why he was getting up, but he was grateful for it. He'd finally gotten up and close with her. Plus, she was holding him.

"You fell out." She chuckled.

At that point, he became a little embarrassed. How could his first impression be that of all things? The last thing he wanted was to look stupid in front of her, the girl of his dreams, although he'd find out it would be worth it.

They became good friends and then boyfriend-girlfriend. For months, he felt a happiness he'd never experienced before. Everything was perfect, placing him on top of the world until one Thursday afternoon.

While sitting at Mesha's house, on the back porch playing spades, D-nice was having fun winning until he caught something odd in his peripheral. Mesha stood off to the side of them, gripping her chest tightly with an expression across her face that said something was wrong.

"Mesha!" D-nice yelled out. He was concerned but not fully aware of the serious condition that was taking hold of her.

Her face balled up like she'd been in horrible pain. Then, she collapsed to the wood beneath her, trembling as life slowly escaped her body.

"Mesha!" he shouted louder, kneeling down beside her, confused and on the verge of becoming hysterical. Panic creeped up his spine, shaking every bone in his body as it continued to go up and up. *What's wrong*? His mind screamed over and over while he stared down on the gasping love of his life.

Her gasps for air became harder, deeper, heavier. Her body began to quake sporadically with a tear finding its way down her face, matching the ebb of the ones sliding down D-nice's.

He wanted to do something – hell, anything – to stop whatever it was, but his mind roamed in a blank realm. Every piece of existence had faded away besides that of her jerking torso.

Then, suddenly, he'd been brought back to reality. "Move the hell out the way. Mesha, baby?" her father said, slinging D-nice from over her.

Falling on his behind, D-nice stared in disbelief as her father's screams for help shook his core.

"Why the hell you sitting there? Go and get some help," he shouted at D-nice, glaring like he'd caused it.

Scrambling to his feet in desperation would be the last thing he remembered of that dreadful day, the day love was snatched from him by nothing less than the heart itself. For days, he cried and cried, pleading with God to bring her back. Yet it would be to no avail. His words and promises had only fallen upon deaf ears, which lead him into a state of disbelief in such a thing as *God*. He forced himself to leave his love with Mesha on the day she was lowered into the earth.

Now – years later – here he was, wholeheartedly avoiding both at all costs, refusing to let any preacher convince him of a savior or any female seduce him into a love lock.

Ace and the crew would sometimes try and encourage him to indulge in somebody, telling him over and over that, "everybody needs somebody." Whereas he'd return, "I got y'all and… Pamela,"' and laugh with the wave of his hand.

Biting down on his bottom lip, D-nice tightened his grip around his manhood, stroking it harder and wildly while keeping his focus on the thick, Asian chick who was taking more dick than she probably agreed to. Damn, he was feeling it, almost to the point of exploding, then everything went black.

"The fuck!" he hissed, trying to adjust his retinas in the darkness.

Quickly, and caring less about the grease on his hands, he snatched up his pants then the Mack 11 which had been laying on the side of him.

He swept his eyes in the darkness from left to right before he took a step in the direction of the breaker. Moving to and through the hallway, D-nice felt along the wall with his free hand until he reached the metal cover of it. He didn't have to make sure he located it because there was nothing else like it. Feeling the latch, he pulled it open. This was the tricky part though. He never memorized the switches, so he switched all of them right to left like he sometimes did at Ms. Shirley's house when he'd blown the power from too many things running at the same time.

However, still nothing happened, which caused him to switch it again. He did so and got the same result.

"Fuck!" he growled, realizing now that something more serious than a mere outage had caused it.

Quickly, he reversed, stepping the way he'd come from until his hand grasped the front door's handle. Pulling the door to a crack, he peered out at the street, studying it closely like he'd always done before leaving the confinement of the spot. He'd instantly be paranoid by anything which wasn't part of the ordinary picture.

All good, he said to himself, leaping from the porch and heading straight for the side of the house. He used the little rays of light that came from the streetlights as a guide. He continued to move along the side, halting at a black box mounted onto the side.

Using his index finger, he felt for the latch. He was about to pull it open until he noticed something out of place. Thanks to the dim lighting, he could see that the wires which ran out of the top had been cut intentionally.

His hand clutched the Mack 11 tighter as he ran his fingers over the severed edges. Then, he heard a clicking sound behind him, followed by a voice. "Move and you die."

The words sent a cold shiver through his bones. How could he have slipped this bad?

Damn, he cursed himself, feeling the cold steel press against the nape of his neck.

D-nice gritted his golds, letting his finger caress the trigger, wanting badly to try whomever the fuck it was behind him. He decided though that would probably be a bad move due to his ears catching every syllable of dude's next choice of words. "You must really wanna die tonight?"

"Who's to say you won't kill me anyway?" D-nice asked, clearly understanding the reality of his statement. These days, he knew it was very unlikely that a nigga would make it out of a situation like this, especially when you were on the wrong side of the muzzle.

"That a be left up to you," the visitor told him before giving him directions to release his weapon.

"I guess," D-nice retorted, letting the Mack collide with the ground. Any other time or situation, he would have taken his chances, but he could see that this particular stranger was no average street nigga. Street niggas were a lot more aggressive, more sporadic. They didn't waste time sounding calm like they had common sense, which was rare amongst most of them.

"That a boy," exclaimed the visitor, running his free hand around D-nice's waistline, searching for anything else. "Now, put your hands in the back of you."

D-nice complied gladly, thinking that if dude intended on tying his hands with anything, he would have to lower his gun to do so, presenting the perfect opportunity to try something. His swift plot quickly faded to nothing. The sound of feet shuffling toward him from somewhere behind caught his attention.

More than one, he now knew. Those moving feet didn't belong to the one with the pistol still in its exact place on his neck. Within a split second, he felt plastic on his skin, then he heard the clicking sound as the zip ties tightened around his wrists, binding them.

"Let's go," commanded the visitor, grabbing him by the back of his neck and pivoting him around.

"Where we going?" D-nice asked, being funny.

"To the club. Where the fuck you think?" He pushed D-nice forward.

Thoughts ran through D-nice's mind, causing him to smile. How in the fuck were they going to see in the spot when all the power had been cut, thanks to their very own doing? D-nice stopped just beyond the threshold of the doorway.

"What? You afraid of the dark?" The visitor chuckled.

"Kind of."

The guy laughed. "Smart ass." He then pushed the barrel of his gun harder into his neck. "The next one will be your last one, get it?"

"Yeah," D-nice managed in a low grumble. D-nice took small steps, unable to see. He wondered how they expected to accomplish whatever had been on their minds. These fucking geniuses had cut all the lights off.

Stepping into the living room, it seemed darker than he remembered. Maybe it was because, at first, he'd been alone, but now, he was tied up with unwelcome armed guests.

"Who else is here?" whispered the visitor, getting closer to his ear.

"Nobody," D-nice whispered back, mocking his new friend.

"Good." The guy laughed again, slightly amused. "If you be a good boy, we'll be outta here in no time."

"Hopefully." D-nice didn't mean to say that out loud. Sometimes pressured situations caused thoughts to slip from people's lips.

Maneuvering D-nice with his hand, he told him, "Take a seat." He then slapped him in the side of the head with the pistol, causing him to spit out a little grunt as he crashed into the wood floor.

"Fuck!" he barked in pain, a little dizzy from the blow.

He felt the dude's knee press down on his neck. "Now, tell me where the money is." The sound of his words displayed that a new demon had kicked in.

"What?" D-nice shot back, never thinking he'd feel his own blood pool under his face.

"The money?"

"What money?"

"The fucking money you and your little homeboys been stacking up in here."

"Man, we don't keep shit in here." D-nice tried to sound sincere through the throbbing of his skull. It felt like he was about to pass out.

"It's funny you say that because I been hearing otherwise." The visitor applied more pressure down on his neck, forcing an agonizing growl to escape D-nice's lips. "Now, we can either do this the easy way, and you give us what we came for, or…" He paused, pulling on D-nice's arms, using it as leverage to add a little more pressure. "Or we can do this the hard way, which will be you taking whatever I can think of to dish. Trust me, it would be nothing compared to what you just felt. I know exactly how to make it a long night."

D-nice clenched his teeth from the pain as the copper smell of his own blood filled his nostrils. Enduring the pain, thoughts went in and out of his mind about how and how not to handle this. However, he wouldn't have a chance to deeply contemplate it.

"Okay, the hard way it is." Then, dude lifted up, positioning himself directly over D-nice.

Lifting D-nice by the neck, he was about to strike him again until he pleaded, "Aight, aight, man, I got you."

Once the guy released him, he knew that no matter what he said, they wouldn't be able to see in the dark. The entire house was pitch black, but he'd leave that to them to figure out.

"Look in the bathroom…" Damn, D-nice didn't want to tell them, but neither did he want to die like this. There was always the chance that they'd be able to find them and get it all back with a little revenge for his pain.

"Where in the bathroom?" He could easily hear it in the man's voice that he was becoming irritably impatient.

D-nice laid his head back down in his own blood, already regretting the choice he was about to make. "In the floor… up-up under the sink," he stuttered on the verge of fainting.

"Check it out," the dude said to his anonymous protégé. Then, D-nice listened to footsteps move away and toward the designated area. "Mind if I ask you something while we wait?" the guy asked him, like he'd regained his previous *calm* composure.

Is this nigga serious? D-nice couldn't help but to wonder, moving his head a little bit to keep his own fluids from getting into his eye.

"Let me get that," he said, moving D-nice away from the puddle, smudging the crimson down his cheek.

D-nice stared up at the dark figure, trying to figure out how in the hell he knew the blood was right there. He knew it was very impossible for anybody to see that good in the dark. But then it made sense. They were, or had to be, wearing night vision goggles. That would explain everything behind them killing all the lights. These muthafuckas were smart.

"So, tell me," he began, sliding the light coffee table over to sit on it, "how much exactly is Ace bringing in nowadays?"

"Ace?" D-nice played as if the name was foreign to him. There was no way he'd put Ace in a fucked-up position. He was way too loyal for that.

"Yeah, Ace… the pretty boy muthafucker with all the tattoos. You know, the guy running this whole little set up."

"Nah, I run this," D-nice said, wondering how long these niggas had been watching them.

"No, no, no. He's the boss. You're the worker. Unless you was the one Black raised?"

Damn, dude has really done his homework. Had to unless…

"Okay, let me put it this way – and maybe you'd understand the depth of my knowledge then. Him and his new jail buddy are the ones who killed Mal. Does that name ring a bell?"

"So, Black sent y'all muthafuckas?" D-nice snarled, knowing they should have been taken it to that nigga's ass a long time ago.

"Black?" The guy laughed, amused. "Yeah, that's exactly who sent us."

"What's so funny?" D-nice wanted to know why that was so funny.

"Nothing. Well, it's just that…" His words were cut short by the rejoining of his partner.

"Got it."

D-nice glanced in the direction where he knew the hallway to be, wishing he could penetrate the pitch blackness. He prayed he'd been wrong about what he said but knew it was true. What else would he find, some water pipes?

Then, out of nowhere, a third voice resonated through the dark, causing him to become shocked. The entire time, he wasn't aware of a third presence, especially that of a woman.

"What we gone do with him?" she questioned, sounding like she was either standing at the front door or kitchen.

His mind had been so caught up on the voice that the thought hadn't registered in his head until seconds later as to what she was implying.

"What you think?" the guy returned casually, like it didn't matter to him one bit.

"Well, do whatever you feel is necessary, just hurry up so we can be on our fucking way," she said, her feet sounding like they were receding.

D-nice listened, understanding at this point that he'd be dead in a few seconds. "Fuck it," he mumbled under his breath, but it was still audible.

"What's that?" the visitor asked, kicking the small table away.

"Shid, I know what's up. Just know Ace gone find y'all… and my nigga when he do…" He began to laugh as he spoke his final words. "Remember, I told you so."

There was a brief pause between the two of them. Nothing was heard besides another person's footsteps treading across the wooden floor.

"Sure," the guy returned calmly.

D-nice closed his eyes, ready to let life take its course. Within that same second, he felt the last pain he would never get to feel again to the side of his head.

CHAPTER ONE

"Ace, bra, I've always said ain't gone let no cowards kill me. Fuck I look like, Scarface?" Whiteboy chuckled slightly, sitting at the table.

Ace managed to bring a half smile to his face through the tears that streamed recklessly down his face. He couldn't help but to stare at his brother – his best friend – who'd been shot multiple times in the shootout they'd barely made it through.

No more than thirty minutes ago, they'd left a meeting with a rival, which both parties had parted on bad terms. What could he say? The terms they were trying to offer were non-negotiable. It was what it was.

Fifteen minutes ago, they were sitting at a red light, contemplating what their next move was to be if they planned on making it through the next few weeks with their lives.

Opinions had been tossed around when they'd left the meeting and were still being thrown around when they were flanked by two SUVs.

Before they even had the slightest chance to react, the trucks stopped on the sides of them, muzzles pointed in their direction.

Gunfire erupted, and Ace's foot was too slow in hitting the accelerator. They were getting shot, and they were shooting back, Whiteboy squeezing his hammer mostly. Ace had to maneuver them out of this tight situation.

God had been with them. They'd made it out – somewhat. Now, here the two of them sat at Missy's kitchen table, Ace's shoulder grazed by a bullet and Whiteboy with more than eight beneath his flesh.

"Shawty…" Whiteboy began, staring at Ace, his brother, watching him in tears. "We done came a long way together, but…"

"But shit. We still got a way to go, nigga," Ace snapped. He was nowhere near ready to accept the inevitable. Damn, he wanted to kill them all.

"Nah… you do," were Whiteboy's last words before he lifted the pistol to his own temple.

"*Noooo!!!*"

"Ace! Ace!" he heard loudly through the darkness. Opening his eyes, he saw the love of his life leaning over him. "Baby, you okay?"

Taking a deep swallow, he uttered dryly, "Yeah." He wasn't sure though. His heart was pounding hard against the inside of his chest. His insides felt as if they'd pushed his lungs into his throat.

"You sure?"

"Yeah, I'm good. Just another one of them dreams," he said, pulling the covers from over him and stepping out of the bed. Lately, he'd been experiencing similar dreams, and the more he encountered them, the closer to reality they would seem.

He couldn't understand it. First, he'd be engaging some unknowns in pistol play, who always shot him down. More recently, the events changed from him to different people in his life ending up on death's doorstep, being issued what was obviously meant for him.

What is it all supposed to mean? he asked himself, staring at the water flowing from the bathroom's faucet. He splashed his face twice then gazed up at his dripping reflection, watching the liquid make streams down his face.

"Nigga, get a grip," he told himself, cutting the water and light off as he made his exit.

The dream continued to replay itself over and over within his head as he walked through the threshold of the bedroom he shared with Sassy.

Heading for the kitchen, he told himself, *Whiteboy wouldn't do no stupid shit like that.* He hoped that his dream was as fake as the others. Ace had to reassure himself though. He knew there really was no fucking telling fucking with his crazy ass protégé.

Taking the liter of orange juice from the refrigerator, he poured up a glass, and then, his phone went off.

You niggas are some real live peons. The music played as loud as ever, as if it was in desperate need of his attention.

Leaving it on the charger in the living room was something he'd been forced to do, thanks to the complaining Sassy. She would whimper and rant every time it blared in the middle of the night. People would call throughout the night for reasons minor to her but important to him.

Smiling, Ace stepped over to it. He looked at it. This had been the call he'd been waiting on. He wanted badly to hear the voice on the other end, especially after knowing what he'd done to Mal. And *how* he'd done it to Mal.

"Yeah..." he answered nonchalantly.

Black laughed. "Ace, you grew a lot of fucking balls, huh? I mean, what? You think a nigga ain't going to get retribution, lil nigga?"

"Nigga, I'm waiting."

"I hope you is," he said in a menacing chuckle. "I hope you ready to see your whole fucking little clique dead. I'm not going to stop until every last one of y'all are fucking stepped on."

"Yeah, aight." Ace smiled, wishing the two of them were face-to-face. He wanted to see how much of that shit he would back up.

"All the shit I did for you, lil nigga, and this how the fuck you wanna repay me!"

"Nigga, fuck you! You ain't did shit but fuck over a nigga."

"Fuck over you? Lil bitch, I gave you more than you ever thought about having. Fuck is you talking about? Nigga, I fed you when yen have a muthafucking thing to eat. Gave you a place to stay when yo lil bum ass was sleeping outside…"

"Yeah, just so you could fuck over Missy."

"Ha! Nigga, ain't nobody fuck over that bitch. Her cancer infested ass begged for the dick."

His words stung Ace to the core, causing him to squeeze his touchscreen to the point of cracking. *Fuck!* he cursed himself, ready to dead Black and whoever else at this point. He'd hit a nerve, and Ace wanted to express exactly how hard he'd hit it.

"Nigga, I want you to know that that bitch gone be the reason you end up like that nigga, Mal."

"Ace, be for real. Nigga, you know who the fuck I am so miss me with that weak shit. I'll be to see you though, lil nigga."

"Likewise," was Ace's last word before the call disconnected. Heated, Ace tossed the phone to the couch and turned, only to realize that Sassy was standing at the foot of the hallway.

"Who was that?" she asked, wiping the sleep from her eyes.

"Look, right…" Ace began, flatly ignoring her question. "I want you to holla at Latoya and see if she wanna go out of town with you for a few days." He had already pondered over ways to tell her this days ago. He could never think of the right way, and at this point, it wouldn't matter. Shit was about to get real, and he refused to have her anywhere near it. That was out of the question.

"Out of town?" She became perplexed, not understanding. "Baby, what's going on?"

He continued to ignore her questions. There was no need to entertain them. His mind was made up. "I'ma go to the spot, get you a couple of bands. Ten or fifteen should be enough to hold y'all down, aight?"

"Ace, what's going on? Why can't I stay here?" She wanted to know as her attitude began to creep its way onto the scene.

"It ain't safe," he barked, brushing past her, though not meaning the bump to be so aggressive. But she was in the way and wasn't listening.

"Why ain't it? Don't nobody know where we stay… or do they?"

"No!"

"So, why do I need to go out of town, Ace?"

"Just in case, man, damn!"

"Just in case what?" She just couldn't let it go. Something was terribly wrong, and she was determined to know if Ace was in trouble – if they were.

Ace huffed a deep breath. "Man, listen… Just do what the fuck I tell you, aight?" Before he knew it, he had seized her by both arms, grabbing them tightly before snarling, "Aight?" again.

Sassy was speechless for a second, hurt and shook. She had never seen this side of him, no matter how bad she'd get on his nerves. "Okay. Let me go!"

He stared into her brown eyes as they began to tear. *Damn, I'm tripping*, he said to himself, letting her go after realizing his transgression. A lot had happened between them. They had argued, laughed, and argued again, but never had he possessed the audacity to put his hands on her in any way besides a loving way. However, that was then, and this was now. Situations changed all the time, and they both needed to see that.

His glare lightened as she flopped down on the bed. Evidently, she was as confused as he was, just not as much. So many things had made trails through his mind that he had the slightest clue on which course to take. However, there was one thing he did know. He wasn't going to let anything happen to her or his unborn child. That was out of the question. Period.

Being lost on words, he started putting on his clothes. He swept his eyes over to the digital clock on the nightstand, and it read 9:20 a.m.

Shit, it's late, he told himself, still continuing to get himself together. After sliding into his Vans, he reached and pulled the Ruger .45 from under his pillow. Ace gave it an overview, wondering how many lives it would claim before the beef would be settled. There was no telling, and really, he could care less as to how many. He just wanted to be the last one standing when the smoke cleared.

Moving toward the bedroom door, Ace stopped and glanced back at his beautiful life, the reason he would use everything in his power to be the last nigga remaining. She sat motionless, head down, eyes penetrating the carpet.

A second, then two, passed. He didn't know what to say or exactly how to say anything. Maybe he would later. He hoped he would as he turned to leave.

BLACK SAT THERE ON HIS FOREIGN COUCH, OBSERVING THE NEW recruits who he would send to kill Ace for what he'd done to his second-in-command.

Damn, outta all the fucking killers I had on my team, how did I end up with this bunch of trash ass niggas? he asked himself, knowing that if he sent this group that stood before him, for sure Ace would kill all of them. Shid, they would probably be more useful dead anyway.

"Aye, Pee Pee," Black called out, picking up the blunt from the ashtray, admiring it.

"Yo..." Pee Pee responded, more than ready for him to fire up the Kush.

"I want you to lead them in killing Ace." He paused a quick second to fire up the weed. "Take them and ride through East Atlanta by his spot." He inhaled, holding the acrid smoke a few seconds then released. "Flame his ass up and whoever wit 'em. Especially that white muthafucka he playing close."

"Talking bout holmes who did that shit in the living room?" Pee Pee knew exactly who he was talking about, but he wanted him to keep talking, so he could take his time with the weed.

"Exactly. Make sure y'all tear that bitch nigga apart. I'm talking cannibal type shit. That a be his welcome home present," he finished, beginning to laugh.

"Fucking right. I got you, big dog... personally," one of his latest recruits assured him.

Black studied the group again. "Listen," he scooted to the edge of the couch, "if all go well today, I got some big shit lined up for y'all. But only for the niggas who prove themselves. Show me y'all gonna eat, and I don't mean on no halfway type shit. I mean eat like the fucking wolves do. Feel me?"

"Hell yeah!" another one of them exclaimed as all nodded their heads in agreement.

"Aight, you niggas step out a minute. Pee Pee, I need to holla at you," Black told them, leaning back against the couch, getting comfortable before taking another drag from the blunt. He watched as the last nigga pulled the door shut then focused his attention on the last two niggas left in the room besides himself.

"Pee Pee, you need to make sure the shit is handled right. Ain got time for war back, especially not with a shipment coming in…" He paused, taking more smoke into his lungs. "You got to make it a one shot, one kill thing, aight?" Black finished, passing the weed to him.

"Reno," he gazed across at him, "what your people talking about?"

Reno was quiet a moment. Hearing him talk about Ace's death had put him in a trance, like it always did. All he wanted was for that nigga to die–die–die.

Many times, he'd contemplated Ace's demise. Now – finally – it was about to take place, and he couldn't wait. However, he felt a little jealous because he wanted to be the one responsible for sending that final bullet into his skull, which would send him away forever.

"Reno!" Black shouted, getting his attention.

"Yeah, big bra," Reno quickly returned, finding it hard to force Ace to the back of his mind.

"You heard me?"

"Yeah."

"What I say then?" questioned Black, skeptical.

"Some'n bout my people," Reno uttered stupidly.

"Nigga, I asked what yo people talking about," he snapped, wondering what the hell had been up with him lately. He'd been acting a little odd.

"Oh, shid, whenever you get right, they ready."

"Um…" Black swept his gaze from Reno to Pee Pee then back before taking another pull. "Just like that?" he emphasized, snapping his fingers.

"Yeah, I guess. That's what they said."

"Nigga, I don't need you to fucking guess. I need a fo sho."

"Bra, I can only tell you what they tell me."

"Well, you need to holla at them and make sure cause if they bull-shitting – wasting a nigga's time – then they ass just as dead as Ace. Real shit." Black stared him down as if to say he would be too if it came down to that.

"Ye-yeah, big bra," Reno stuttered, standing more than ready to make an exit. "I'll hit once I get word."

"Yeah, do that," Black spit out toward his back as he left. "Pee Pee," he whispered, causing Pee Pee to lean toward him. "My nigga, something ain't right with that shit. Ion know what it is, but it's some-thing going on, and ion like it. First shit don't go as expected, kill that fool," he finished, tilting his head toward the door.

"Say less," said Pee Pee, realizing now that he wasn't the only one suspicious about Reno. Something just wasn't right with him.

CHAPTER TWO

Damn, bae, I'm sorry. Ace rubbed his hand across his face, feeling like a bag of shit. Surely, he'd tripped out. *But sometimes, she has to learn just to do what the fuck I say,* he thought, eyes on the elevator's display. He watched the numbers slowly drop.

Bing! The sound was louder than he'd remembered – or thought he remembered. He wasn't for sure because he never really paid attention to simple things like that.

Stopping on the ground floor, Ace glanced around the lobby as he moved through and out of the double doors.

How could he have let that shit interfere with his home? He knew that you weren't supposed to ever bring the streets into your home because, once they were in, the problems would mix and never dissolve.

However, her leaving was for the best, like just in case niggas knew where he laid his head, which he doubted. Plus, there was no such thing as being overly cautious, especially when it came to his family or soon to be family.

And if nothing else, that nigga, Black, was more than aware of how to break him. Ace could see her already in his sights, Black plotting on how he would find her just to hurt him, and there was no way in fuck he'd let that happen. He'd die first, which had been a part of the plan anyway if he failed at killing Black first.

His phone blared to life in his pocket as soon as he reached the front of his Benz. Pulling it out, Ace read the screen. *Who?* he had to ask himself because he'd cracked the screen to the extent that now the number couldn't be made out, even though it continued to light up.

"Fuck!" he yelled out, mad but a little grateful that he could still touch the bottom and answer it. "Yo..." he answered, praying that nothing else had malfunctioned on the device.

"Man, where you at?" Whiteboy questioned like always.

"Nigga, where you?" Ace asked smartly.

"Man, stop playing, shawty. I been up like since seven-thirty waiting on you."

"Aight then, nigga, continue to wait. I'll be there in a minute."

"Man, aight," Whiteboy huffed, annoyed.

Ace chuckled at this nigga sounding like a child. "Nigga, learn to have some patience."

"Man, fuck all that, just come on."

"Bye!" Ace finished, pressing down hard on the touchscreen, unable to see what the hell he was doing. Damn, he'd have to buy another phone today.

Hitting the push button on his key ring, he listened to the car crank then hopped in. For some odd reason, every time he got in the muthafucka, it would feel new to him. Maybe it was because it still had the new scent. But whatever it was, he wished it remained this way.

Tossing the phone to the passenger side seat, he slapped in 50 Cent's *Massacre* CD and pulled out of the loft's parking lot.

"Niggas screw their face up at me..." Ace continued rapping along as he weaved in and out of the traffic in 4th Ward, glancing at the lil females and lames of the area. He couldn't see how they were posted up in this hot ass sun with nothing better to do with their time.

"Pitiful," he said, rolling down the strip, trying to avoid the gazes of a few local hoes he smashed a time ago. Some he'd fucked just because of the whip he pushed, but how could he be mad at that? If any bitch wanted his time, they'd have to pay for it. He wasn't the average Joe Blow anymore. His game had stepped up and so had his perspective.

Coming to a stop at the red light, Ace's eyes spotted a black tinted out truck two cars behind. He'd noticed that it made the same last few turns as he had.

I might be tripping, he began to think, still closely watching it in his rearview mirror. He tried his best to get a glimpse of who the fuck rode in it.

Buuummmm! The sound of a horn startled him. Quickly, he glanced up at the light, which was now green. Ace pressed down on the accelerator. He decided to find out if these niggas were actually tailing him.

Pushing past the light, he drove past the next intersection, making a right. Slowing his vehicle, his attention stayed on the truck that was still a short distance behind. It turned and imitated exactly what Ace had done.

"Okay. Let's get it then," he growled, hitting the gas, forcing the Benz to snatch forward down the street. He watched the SUV pick up speed as well. Ace slowed, making a quick left, punching it into the nearest parking lot.

Slamming down on the brakes, the car slid to a screeching stop. He slung the door open after grabbing the Ruger .45 from the floorboard. No hesitation, he quickly sprinted to the end of the parking lot, snatching back the slide. He was ready to see the truck turn the corner. As soon as it did, he wouldn't waste any time in knocking the doors off that bitch.

A few feet away, he heard feet shuffling across the asphalt. Speedily, he pivoted around to see two young females walking across the street in an attempt to avoid him.

He guessed they'd seen the gun, which was enough for anybody to want to get away from. Ace put his attention back on the street. For some odd reason, the truck was late on bending the corner nor did it even cross the intersection. *Maybe it stopped after noticing that I peeped them,* he began to muse while heading back to the Benz.

Shutting the door, Ace slammed the car in gear. He smashed out of the parking lot, back toward the intersection, with the pistol still in hand.

Making it back to the corner, he swept his gaze up and down the street. There was no sign of the truck. He looked again, and there was still nothing besides the regular traffic and the females who'd crossed the street, staring at him like he'd lost his mind.

Maybe he was, or was he on his way there?

"Man, chill out with the paranoid shit," he coached himself, unable to explain the shit which had just occurred. He had to think about it, wondering if it had been one of those mirages like he'd seen with Missy.

AN HOUR AND A HALF AFTER THE TRUCK INCIDENT, HE WAS FINALLY pulling up in front of the apartment he had gotten for Whiteboy in Lithonia. He felt it was better for him to be out toward this way than near all the hood shit. Surely this nigga would find trouble, and only more problems would follow. So, the farther the better.

"I know this nigga mad as hell." He chuckled to himself, jumping from the car. Glancing around, he saw there wasn't a being in sight. *Perfect for 'em.* Ace smiled as he headed up the building's stairs to door sixteen eleven.

Pounding on the door four hard ass times, Ace smiled. He knew what this nigga's mood would be like.

"Who is it?" Whiteboy questioned suspiciously from the other side of the door.

"This dick, nigga. Open the fucking door."

"Nigga, nah… Wait like I had to!"

"Cool. I'll be back later then," Ace told him, playing like he was about to walk off and leave. Before he could even make it down the first step, he caught wind of the door unlocking.

"Shid, nigga, you ain't finna leave me," Whiteboy said, flying from beyond the threshold.

"Man, slow the fuck down. Ain't nobody bout to leave yo stupid ass." Ace laughed, watching Whiteboy struggle trying to slide on his left shoe.

"Man, what the hell took you so long?"

"I had to stop and get another phone," Ace said, waving his new iPhone in front of him.

"Nice. You must have got tired of the *new*, old shit?" Whiteboy joked, knowing his bro kept nothing less than top of the line shit. They were things he was ready to possess as well.

"Broke it this morning."

"Damn, how?"

"I need anger management." Ace chuckled, thinking that he was definitely going to need it after doing what he planned on doing to Black.

"Angry ass." Whiteboy laughed, stepping off.

"Look who's talking." Ace pushed him slightly, then he felt his phone vibrate.

"Yo..." he answered, descending down the stairs. "What?" He stopped at the bottom. For some reason, he was expecting to see the truck from two hours ago, which was still nowhere in sight. "He not there? Hit his phone and see what the hell he got going on," Ace said.

"What's up?" Whiteboy became curious by the expression he displayed.

Ace put up one finger, still listening to Ariel. "Well, I'ma hit 'em. He tripping. But look, me and White got some'n to handle so hit Kero. He got a key. Aight," were his last words before he hung up. Luckily, he'd transferred all of his contacts because he didn't know anybody's number by heart.

"What's going on?" Whiteboy, for some reason, was desperate to know.

Scrolling through his contacts, he found the number he'd been looking for. "This nigga, D-nice, done left the spot and ain't tell nobody shit," Ace told him, listening to D-nice's ring back then his voicemail. "Say, Nice, pick the fucking phone up, nigga."

"He might of went to his spot."

"Nigga, that is his spot. That nigga stay there." Ace dialed his number a second time and got the same result. He pulled open the door to the Benz.

"Oh, so what we about to handle?" Whiteboy asked, more focused on going through Ace's CDs than on what he was about to say.

"Shid, what you been wanting to do your whole bid?" Ace watched the reaction to his statement and had no doubt after that.

Whiteboy caught his drift because he only had one thing to handle. He began to nod his head up and down. The time had come.

"What bra say? He talked to him?" Dre asked Ariel, who'd just gotten off the phone with Ace.

"Nothing and no. He ain't talked to his ass. He told me to call Kero; he got a key. But ain't no telling where he at..." Ariel pulled his number up and pressed to call.

"I know that's right. He probably somewhere eating some dry pussy." Dre laughed, knowing Kero's freaky ass.

"Or some dry ass!" Ariel snickered, listening to the music play while she waited on him to pick up. Even though she knew all Kero wanted to do was fuck hoes, it would never stop him from placing the team before a nut. "It's too hot for this shit," she huffed, about to scream at the ring back.

"I'm telling ya," Dre agreed, ready to break in the spot, but he knew Ace would be mad as hell. "If he ain't picking up either, then him and Nice must be together," he assumed until he heard Ariel's voice.

"Kero, where you at? Is Nice with you?" she asked, glancing over at Dre, hoping they were together. It was odd for D-nice to leave the spot. Hell, she couldn't remember a time when he wasn't there. "Cause his ass ain't in the spot, or he ain't answering his phone... Kero, didn't I just say we don't know? If we did, I wouldn't be calling you, stupid... Aight, just try to hurry. I'm losing money playing this *Hide and Seek* game... Fuck you!" she snarled into the phone, ending the call before glancing up at Dre.

"What?" he asked with a curious facial expression.

"Nothing. He make me sick with all that nasty shit." She shook her head, disgusted.

Dre smiled. "Well, stop playing wit that lil shit and let 'em try it out."

"Nigga, he wouldn't get this pussy if I had to choose between fucking him or a rabid dog."

"Oh, so you saying you like it doggy style." He laughed.

"Dre, I'ma let you have that."

"Shid, I'm saying, you the one talking bout fucking dogs and shit. You a animal raper?" He laughed harder.

"Nigga, you the animal raper. Fucking that gorilla looking bitch, Washy." Ariel laughed, imitating the movements and sounds of one.

"Man, go head on." Dre chuckled, hating the fact that he'd ever said something and now wished he never brought her around them. Ever since the first time they saw her, they'd been taking her ass out with the *Willie B* jokes. To him, she was the best fuck ever.

"Keep it real, Dre. So, you don't be thinking about no monkey while fucking her?" she asked with a slight laugh.

"Fuck you, girl!" He laughed, playfully pushing her.

"I know that's right." She giggled.

Covering his eyes, Dre gazed up toward the sun. "Man, it's too hot for this bullshit." It seemed to be getting hotter, which was his reason for heading for his truck.

"Where you about to go?"

"Shid, finna go grab something to chew on. You riding?" he questioned.

"I'm not finna stay here," she said, grabbing her purse and locking up her Lexus.

"Any more *Washy–Monkey* jokes, you will."

"Nigga, please, and don't forget I got a car too." Ariel sexily pointed at the red Lex.

"Well, use it then, nigga." Dre hopped in the driver's seat, deciding whether or not to unlock the passenger door.

"Why when I got a big, healthy chauffeur?" She smiled, pulling on the door handle, only to see that it was locked. She gave him her best baby doll look.

"Like hell," he said and waited a few more seconds before letting her in.

Snatching open the door, she placed one foot on the truck's floor-board, instantly noticing a light smudge of dirt on her stiletto, something her type didn't tolerate, period. She always made sure that her appearance spoke nothing less than *classy ass bitch* from head to toe. There wasn't time for the *classy* part to be subtracted due to a small anomaly. No, everything needed to be perfect and at all times.

Licking her thumb slightly, she knelt a bit to erase the disgrace. Then, in that very moment, she caught the sound of a loud rumbling.

Her head snapped up out of instinct. Ariel glanced backwards at the spot and then at the two houses on the sides. Nothing moved, which she expected. It had been too close to come from either of them. Plus, the pit of her stomach was telling her that whatever it was that made the noise was in the spot. How and what it was perplexed her.

"Dre?" she called out lowly, still staring at the house. "Dre..." she growled a little louder, making a complete three sixty.

"What?" he questioned, raising his eyes from his phone.

"I think I heard something," she said, studying the property closely.

"I mean, when you're outside, you gone hear shit," he said, being funny.

"No, stupid. I think I heard something in there," she told him suspiciously, tilting her head toward the spot.

Hopping out of the SUV, Dre followed her lead up to the front porch. Ariel pressed her ear to the door and listened. At first, there was nothing besides the depths of silence. Then, within a split second, another thump occurred.

"See..." she lowly said to Dre, who now heard it as well. Without any hesitation, Dre lifted his t-shirt, snatching the nine-millimeter Beretta from his waistline. He began to think that it could have been some jay ass nigga who'd broken in. And if so, surely this would be the last premise he invaded.

"Ariel, watch the front. I'ma go round back and see if a nigga broke in," Dre stated, quickly leaping from the porch, creeping around the side of the house. His eyes swept along the house attentively, searching for anything out of the ordinary. Then, he noticed the wires coming out of the breaker box had been cut. He examined them closely, realizing that they hadn't been snatched apart but sliced on purpose. The edges were smooth, meaning they used something very sharp.

A smile spread across his face, like it always had done when he felt it was time to detonate a muthafucka. Moving along, he began to search for the burglar's entry point. Most definitely he would enter the exact same way.

"Fuck," D-nice grumbled, head pounding with excruciating pain. His hands trembled badly as he attempted to pull himself up using the edge of the coffee table, which did nothing but turn over from his weight.

"Fuck!" he moaned again, trying his best to focus. He stared at his arms as they shook badly, seeming as if they couldn't function right. Something was wrong, but he couldn't figure out how or why he'd been laying here.

Taking his time now with his face down, he slowly dragged his knees up under him while pushing upward on his shaking limbs. Finally, he steadied himself.

He shut his eye lids in hopes of blocking some of the pain that was beating terribly at the front of his skull. Damn, it felt like something had been slammed against the back of his cranium, forcing everything into a tight bundle at the front – everything which now seemed to want to exit.

Controlling his breath, D-nice sat another moment, trying to get it together – rather needing to get it together. He needed to remember what occurred and why, but he couldn't. Nothing besides a cloud of vagueness filled his memory.

Feeling a foreign substance, he reopened his eyes, letting them fall to his hands. Dried, crimson-colored flakes peeled off at certain parts of them. Upon lifting them, he quickly noticed the slashes on his wrists where a good amount of the blood had spewed from. Something had to have been awfully tight to cut into flesh the way it did.

Continuing to stare at the injuries brought back quick, vivid flashes from the night before. It was coming back into his mental. He remembered standing outside for some reason. Then, someone was behind him, shoving a pistol into the back of his head. His mind skipped around a little and stopped at something clasping tightly around his wrists. Then blankness.

"What the hell happened?" he muttered to himself, trying to piece together the unsettling scene. It dawned on him that a stranger had ambushed him, bound him. The realization sent a chill down his spine. In situations involving guns and restraints, death lurked nearby. Its presence loomed, yet he remained inexplicably alive. Why hadn't his luck ran out?"

"Damn," he moaned softly, using two fingers to massage around where the pain was emanating from. There was only the presence of flesh, which was still moist. Quickly, he snatched them away. The two were coated with blood. *Shit*. He wondered if maybe he'd been left for dead and somehow survived the fatal blow.

This, he wanted to smile for, though the pain wouldn't allow it just yet. The reality of the situation wouldn't either. Left for dead but alive and still bleeding. If he didn't do something about it, then surely the strangers' intentions would be accomplished.

Before he had a chance to muse over what to do next, a loud banging sound emitted from somewhere in the back of the house.

Instantly, his mind began to race, sending him into a panicked state. D-nice began to believe that whoever had done this to him was still present somewhere in the house, probably ready to finish the job. It was a job he wasn't ready to let be done, even in his current condition.

Depending on his last bout of strength, D-nice crawled to the nearest wall and used it as leverage to get off the floor. To him, it seemed like the closer he got to getting up, the more whoever it was tried to get to him.

If only dude caught him right now, it would be to his disadvantage.

Anybody would see that he was too weak to do anything, even help his own self, let alone fend an aggressor off. There had been times when a few niggas had him down bad, on the verge of ending him, but in neither situation did they ever come close to actually doing it. His current predicament made him feel more vulnerable than he'd ever felt in his entire life.

Coming to both feet with the wall aiding his stance, D-nice glanced around the living area, searching for anything which could be used in his defense. The intruder was here, and nothing he saw would work besides a small lamp over in the corner, an object he didn't have the strength to handle.

"Shit..." he uttered , sotto voce. The pain escalated higher. He attempted to black it out, but it was too much. Though that wouldn't prevent him from trying to save his life. He looked over the room again. There was nothing. But something else caught his eye. The kitchen was adjacent, and in there, in a particular drawer, laid a baby Glock. It was for unseen situations, exactly like the one at hand.

He inched along the wall toward the opening, aroused by a new motivation that could possibly reverse the inevitable outcome.

Grabbing inside the doorway, he pulled himself through. As soon as he took his second staggering step, an even louder crash echoed throughout the house.

"Man, you gone have to give me a sec!" Kero exclaimed into his phone. Ariel was on the other end. "Aight… let me eat that ass!"

"Who was that?" Spain asked as the two sat in Kero's Challenger SR-T8.

"Ariel. Nice done left the spot, and she mad cause she can't get in." He laughed, lifting the blunt from the ashtray.

Spain chuckled, knowing how Ariel got when she didn't have her way. "I already know she mad as hell."

"Man, what? She fucking heated," Kero returned with another chuckle before firing up the loud and inhaling its sweet taste.

"Already." Spain gazed around at the strange area they were

parked in, somewhere near Buckhead. He was clueless as to where exactly because Kero had taken so many turns and back streets that he couldn't keep track. Hell, the only reason he knew it was near Buckhead was because they'd jumped off the expressway in front of Lenox Mall, and since then, he'd been lost. Never mind that he also didn't know why they were there. There definitely was no telling with Kero.

"Damn..." Kero coughed hard, rocking in his seat. "This shit hitting." He was dying trying to hold the smoke in as he handed the weed to Spain.

Continuing to glance around the wooded scenery, Spain placed it between his lips but paused. "Say, bra, why we sitting out in nowhere?"

"Why? Nosy ass boy."

"Cause, nigga," he paused to make a little room in his lungs, "first off, we the only people out here. And secondly, we been waiting for like damn near an hour, bra."

"And? Nigga, you act like you got some'n better to do." Kero smiled broadly, taking another pull.

"Nigga, I could be doing a thousand other things besides sitting in the middle of the woods waiting on something that might not even show. Especially after an hour done went by." With this, Spain began to wonder why in the hell the parking lot was in the middle of the woods anyway and what the fuck Kero could be trying to handle out here.

On the way out here, he'd noticed a few big ass houses, but there was nothing besides trees and more trees after that until the street became very narrow. It ended with this small parking lot. *Who would of imagined putting a parking lot out here where nothing is?* he was thinking when Kero began to speak.

"One thing bout it, this shit guaranteed, lil nigga, and gone..." he paused briefly to release a cough, "and gone guarantee a lot of more ends real fucking soon. So, if yo young ass be patient and chill, maybe I'll let you in on it," Kero finished, swiping his hand across Spain's forehead, which he knew he hated.

"Nigga, please. Guaranteed? Yeah, we gone be *guaranteed* a bunch of wasted time, exactly like now."

"Shid, you playing. But think of this, right? It's June right now?" he questioned, leading Spain to nod his head in agreement while dumping ashes. "Nigga, by the end of August, I'll be looking at some'n close to a half a mill fucking wit the people I'm fucking with."

"Like who?" Spain asked, now very interested since half a ticket was mentioned. Numbers had a way of doing that to people.

"I can't tell you all that," Kero said nonchalantly, smiling. "Just know they official tissue."

"So, question, do Ace know bout all this?"

"Hell no. Shid, you see how he eating? Bra seeing real paper. That's why he said he really don't give a fuck bout what a nigga do on the side long as it ain't no hot shit and fucking wit his check."

Yeah, but nigga, you talking about half a mill, Spain wanted to tell him. Watching Kero kill the last of the weed, he remained silent. He wondered what he could actually be doing – and with who – to the extent of snatching a half a mill in under two months with no *hot shit* taking place.

Too impossible, he said to himself. He'd never witnessed Kero move any work outside of what Ace was supplying. And if he was, then like everyone in the clique knew, Ace wouldn't understand or accept any part of that, regardless of what he mentioned about the *side shit*.

But then, if it wasn't any blow involved, what would have the potential of producing a half a mill in such a short time span? He had the slightest idea, though he was determined to find out.

"Look at yo thinking ass..." Kero laughed, geeked up. "Yen got to do all that. Just chill and let me do what I does, ya dig? And I'ma make sure you get a nice serving of the plate." Kero leaned over in the seat, staring seriously with his glazed eyes. "And on some real shit, don't tell nobody. I mean, nobody cau..." Before he could finish, a black Yukon swerved into the lot, stopping a few feet away from them. "Let's get it," Kero smiled gladly, quickly exiting.

Spain watched the Yukon with the heavy tint closely. *Who is in it?*

he wondered. Evidently, they didn't want anyone to know who wasn't supposed to, which was probably why Kero walked to the other side to get in. It could have been a truckload for all he knew. Yet a load with those windows could be a crisis in waiting.

Taking no longer than five minutes, Kero reappeared, returning exactly the way he'd come from. He smiled more now as he paced coolly toward his car with a manilla envelope under his arm. Spain only knew one thing that possessed the power to make a person smile like that, and he'd soon see.

The truck was already on its way back up the street by the time Kero yanked the door open, sliding back in.

"Nigga!" he exclaimed excitedly, wasting no time in putting on display the contents of the envelope.

"Damn," Spain uttered, surprised and amazed. His eyes instantly locked in on the stacks of green backs that looked so beautiful.

"Now, that's what the fuck you call *free bandz*," Kero happily shouted, lifting a few of the stacks halfway out.

Spain sat there, watching him close the envelope back, knowing that there were no such thing as *free bandz* unless they miraculously fell out of the sky. However, this money had somehow fallen from a black Yukon.

MAKING IT TO THE BACK OF THE HOUSE, DRE STILL COULDN'T FIGURE out how the intruder had gotten into the spot. He swore he'd checked every entrance, every door, window, vent, and wall. All of it and nothing revealed any evidence of being broken into.

He'd circled the house three times, and two times wondered what he'd missed, but by the third time, he'd finally reached the conclusion that he hadn't missed a damn thing.

So, how in the world did this muthafucka get in? Dre asked himself, studying the back door. He mused over the possibility that whoever it was could have picked the locks. This, in turn, would mean the individual wasn't just another jay from round the way. They had skills, meaning they – more than likely – knew exactly what they were doing and quite possibly to whom.

With that thought, he held up the Beretta, checked the chamber, and stepped toward the door he was for certain he could easily cave in, exactly like he'd done so many others.

Sizing it up, Dre took a short step backwards then launched his thirteen-inch foot. To his surprise, it refused to fall in. Yet its wooden frame cracked along where the hinges were located.

Dre partially smiled before using every bit of his two hundred fifty-five pounds to finish the job. He knew the first kick had alerted whoever it was. The second one, for damn sure, would cause them to prepare for an encounter.

Bringing the gun upward, he stealthily moved beyond the threshold, ready to dead anything which moved. He inched slowly, letting his eyes sweep around the small washroom then toward the dark hallway. At that moment, he was expecting anything to happen.

Peeping, Dre quickly glanced around the edge of the doorway. He listened carefully but didn't hear anything besides the fire detector chirp. He became a little confused. Why wasn't he hearing the intruder trying to escape? Maybe he hadn't retrieved what he came for. Dre smirked, determined to let him leave with something for being stupid and straight up crazy.

Quietly, he shifted his body to the opposite wall, first glancing toward the bathroom, which was near to him. Seeing nothing, his attention peered up the hallway. He stepped but hated the fact that he couldn't prevent the wooden floor from squeaking no matter how softly he laid his feet.

The hallway had been completely drowned in darkness, except for the little rays of sunlight that beamed from the room's windows. This aided him very little, which he wished would be the same for the other person. The last thing he needed was for the adversary to see him first. Damn, that would be bad.

Stopping at the first room, he snuck a brief look. Nothing. He moved a little slower to the next one. Nothing again. Now, all his attention was on the living room and kitchen.

Dre calmed his breathing as he leaned his head forward, one eye creeping past the edge. The blinds let the sun in through its spaces, providing more than enough lighting for him to realize it was like the other rooms. Empty.

His fingers clutched tighter, anticipating the inevitable face-to-face. It was as if the floorboards were anticipating it as well because they had become as silent as ever.

He put his shoulder up against the wall and slid the length until reaching the opening. Holding his breath, a streak of perspiration made its way down the canal of his nose. Dre listened attentively. His ears heard nothing besides his very own heart beating.

Fuck it. With precision, he swung the Beretta around the corner, finger on the trigger and prepared to squeeze it. But he wouldn't. There was nothing there. Like the rest of the house.

"The fuck?" he mumbled in a low growl. Quickly, he spun back around, thinking that he'd missed something. Though he hadn't until he reached the kitchen.

Click, click.

The sound caused him to stop dead in his tracks. *Fuck!* He knew he'd slipped to his own detriment.

"Nigga, stay still," Dre heard. Automatically, he recognized the voice. However, he couldn't understand why in the hell had it been him all along.

"Nice?"

D-nice sat on the floor, in a corner, against the wall of the entrance. What a strategic spot it was.

"Dre?" he finally uttered. His sight had been fucking with him since he'd woken up, but he knew only one person carried that distinctive voice.

"Bra, what the hell you doing?" Dre turned back around yet still couldn't see him, even with squinted eyes. "Man, where you at?"

"Right here," he responded, tapping the pistol against the wall.

Dre's head turned quickly toward the noise. After taking a few steps, he stepped on his foot.

"Ah! Damn, nigga," D-nice barked at his heavy ass protégé.

"Man, what the fuck yo stupid ass doing in the corner? Fucking with them pills again?" Dre asked suspiciously, kneeling down, gripping D-nice's hand, beginning to tug him upward.

"Man, some muthafuckas ran down on me."

"What? What the hell you mean?"

"Ah, shit!" D-nice let out in pain. He couldn't understand how his body had become so sore so quickly.

Moving him to the sofa, Dre let him collapse down on it. "Yeah. Man, shawty, some niggas tied me up last night. I think they tried to kill me."

Tried? Dre began to think curiously. One thing he knew was that if a nigga had you down bad and intended on killing you, the word *tried* didn't exist. Either they did or they didn't. "Tried to kill you?"

Putting his palms up to his head, he said, "Bra, man, ion know." His cranium was still killing him. He really couldn't think right now.

"Hold up, bra." Dre went to the front door and unlocked it for Ariel, who he'd just remembered was outside.

"Say, Ariel," he called out, seeing that she wasn't on the porch anymore. Then, he clicked the light switch, forgetting the smooth disconnection. *Stupid ass*, he called himself, lifting the blinds.

Instantly, D-nice covered his retinas from the blinding sun rays which flooded into the living room. He wanted to curse Dre's ass because this somehow intensified the agonizing pain.

"Nice?" Ariel uttered in wonderment as she walked through the door. "What happened to you?"

She quickly noticed that something was very wrong. Dried blood covered the side of his face and swallowed his hands. As if all of the scenery called for her attention, her eyes fell to the floor where a pool of the same-colored crimson marked its territory. Her stomach twisted into a knot as she glanced over at Dre, who had obviously seen the pool for the first time.

"Shhh..." he returned, shaking his head.

CHAPTER THREE

"**Y**ou ready?" Ace questioned Whiteboy. He'd pulled over a short distance from their destination, needing to know if he was really ready to go through with this.

A few meters away stood the place where it all started, the place Whiteboy had wished to revisit every day and every night that he spent incarcerated. Every day in misery. Every day in sorrow. Every day in pain. The anger and loneliness he'd been forced to face inside during the dreadful confinement. And with each day, he wanted to release that monster which laid deep within the depths of his soul.

Many times, he'd plotted and planned the death of the *sole* reason for him being exposed to the hell that existed behind the prison walls. It was a hell that created and slowly carved him into the beast he became – and later, something worse.

Whiteboy studied the house, which at one time had been his home and later his biggest regret. Nothing changed, he noticed. Every aspect was exactly how he remembered – dirty lawn, trashy porch, crumbling house. Nothing had changed.

"Yeah..." Whiteboy returned, keeping his eyes in place. He always wondered what it would be like once he made it back here. Though as of right now, he felt nothing.

Ace allowed a minor crease to form on his forehead. "Say, you want me to go in with you?" He nonetheless knew the answer to his own question, yet it was his own way of subliminally telling him that once he stepped out of the car, he was on his own and couldn't turn back.

As the Benz crawled to a halt by the walkway, Whiteboy shook his head. He cracked the door open and glanced back at Ace. The grin on his lips conveyed everything he needed to say.

As he treaded along the walkway, a torrent of mixed emotions and memories flooded his mind, fueling the burning rage within him. His heart pounded relentlessly, its rhythm reminiscent of war drums drawing nearer to the battlefield. The sound echoed menacingly through his being, intensifying the already overwhelming rage and fury that consumed him.

Calm down, White, he coached himself. Whiteboy began to feel like a volcano reaching the point of erupting once his feet were planted on the surface of the porch.

Every part of his body became stiff. His mind drifted to the last time he'd actually stood here and how he was taken off of it by the police. It seemed as if the reverie had become a holographic reality, projecting itself right in front of him.

Shaking his mental back to the present, he knocked on the door twice.

I wonder which one of the stupids gone answer? he asked himself, wanting to take a peek through the living room window but thought better of it. This was supposed to be a surprise.

Whiteboy let a couple of seconds pass before crashing his knuckles into it again, this time with a little more force.

"Yeah!" He heard the irritating voice of his mother.

Damn. The last thing he wanted was for her to be the first one on the other side. Though where else would she be? Never had he known of her having a job. This house had been the only place she frequented.

"Who is it?" she yelled. Her voice was louder. Obviously, she stood right up on the door now.

For some strange reason, he felt an urge to smile. But he understood why he couldn't. Another agenda was at play besides that of a happy reunion.

"White..." he told her, pondering over if she even remembered who that name belonged to.

"Who?" she exclaimed, sounding as if she'd been partially surprised. At the same time, it was possible that she hadn't heard him right.

"White, Ma."

With that being spoken, the locks clicked, and the door slowly opened with caution. He, for the first time in years, saw his mother, who looked like she'd recently risen from the bowels of hell. Skin barely hung on to her bones. Her clothes hardly kept hold of flesh, and the dirt had no problems at all clinging onto both. This was a disgusting sight.

She stared at him, not uttering a word. However, if expressions could talk, they would have related a mouthful.

He offered a mild smile, seeing the need to break the cold ice first. "Hey..."

"Hey,'" she said, more like a low huff. She continued to stare in a way that made it seem as if he'd come back from the dead. "When did you get out?"

"Yesterday," he returned flatly. Whiteboy expected her reaction to be something other than this. Why? He didn't know, just did.

"Come in." She finally welcomed him in after another moment of giving him a complete overview.

Stepping inside, Whiteboy's eyes swept over the place quickly. He wanted to laugh. Even after all these years, nothing about it had changed. The scenery had kept its state. Trash covered the carpet. Bottles, cans, and leftover food on dirty dishes still held down the living room table and floor panel TV.

"Cat!" He heard her yell out from behind him as he continued to glance around the disgusting place. Damn, he hated to admit, or believe that, he actually lived here once upon a time. *The prison was way cleaner than this shit,* he thought, causing himself to chuckle. That shit might have been for the best.

"Cat!" she repeated, moving to the hallway to scream his name from the top of her lungs for the second time.

Then, a deep voice yelled back this time. "What?"

It had caused him to stop and remember the only reason he'd even been bothered with the idea of coming back to this dreadful household.

"Come in here. You might want to see this." She smiled, flashing her horribly stained teeth. She snatched the pack of Newports, placing one between her chapped lips.

He just might, Whiteboy thought while watching her light the cigarette, continuing to stare.

"So, what was it like?" his mother asked, letting the acrid smoke swirl upwards from her mouth.

Whiteboy lifted his eyes toward the ceiling, as if to think of the perfect words to describe a hell full of zombies. "Something new," he let out with a slight grin.

With that, she chuckled a bit. "Well, did you learn anything *new* besides being a smart ass?"

"Yeah..." He made eye contact, so she would clearly understand his next words. "I learned how to forgive… and then forget." He continued to stare, realizing it hadn't gone over her head. No, of course not. Her facial expression said it all.

"I guess I deserved that." She dropped her eyes, taking a seat on the sofa. "But like they say… you do the crime, *you* do the time." She added on a sarcastic little laugh.

Really, bitch? he badly wanted to tell her, but the whole purpose of his visit had just appeared from the mouth of the hallway.

Cateye, looking like he'd just woken up, was wiping his eyes. Then, he came to a sudden stop. His father's reaction had been the same as his mother's, disbelieving that he stood in their living room, now fully grown.

Whiteboy stared at his aged father – the father who was responsible for him being locked in a cell of cement, constantly being treated like a fucking animal – the father who had been the reason for all his late-night screams due to the hate, the pain, the agony, and loneliness he was forced to endure day after day. His father was everything which caused him to transform into the mentally challenged monster he had become.

His eyes bore into the man which symbolized the crazy shit he suffered. He was the cause. Whiteboy reminded himself of that every day of his bid. Now he stood face-to-face with the demon of torment.

Cateye remained silent until Whiteboy's mother broke his short daze. "Bae, well, damn, say something," his wife encouraged him.

Another minute went by, then he uttered through his trembling lips. "How you been?"

Whiteboy smiled at the fact that he would even ask something like that. "How I been?" he mocked, trying to keep his composure, more than ready to execute what he'd come to do. "I've been… surviving."

"Oh." Cateye took a seat next to his wife. "It's good to see you in good health."

"Good health?" He offered a laugh. "I mean, you expected something else?"

"Uh, it's just… Damn, boy, it's good to see you make it outta there," Cateye said, actually glad to see that his son had made it out for real.

This nigga got to be joking, Whiteboy thought, letting a weird laugh escape his lips. "Like you cared."

Cateye went silent again. His only child had a point. Hell, he was the one that sent him there, and not one time had he ever wrote or visited him. So, why was he so glad to see the son he apparently hadn't given two fucks about until now? Yet Cateye always knew from that day forward that Whiteboy would hate him with every part of his existence. But he hoped as well that he'd find it somewhere within him to forgive his father for the biggest mistake he'd ever made in his life.

Cateye despised the decision he had made and struggled incessantly to find some semblance of logic to justify his actions. He even sought his wife's perspective, hoping it might shed some light on the situation to make it seem like the right choice. Yet, deep down, he harbored regret, grappling with it every morning when he awoke to find Michael absent from his bedroom, no longer sleeping in his own bed.

How could anyone – let alone a father – turn their child over to a place that would demoralize the innocent essence of the child, throwing them in life-or-death situations daily?

How could I? Cateye asked himself as he gazed at the man who had once been his son, a man who wasn't taught or guided into manhood by his father but became such due to the circumstances of his predicament.

"Micheal…" Cateye began. His expression was pathetic. "I didn't want the street life…" Whiteboy refused to let him finish.

"Don't fucking say it. It means nothing at this point." Whiteboy stared at him. "Every day I sat in there, asking myself why would you do that to me? Why you let them take me? Maybe you didn't fully understand, or didn't want to understand, the sick shit that happens in there every fucking minute of the day.

"Every day having to worry about dying. Every day thinking about what them fucking folks was gone do next to make you feel like shit. Every day wondering when you'd get that visit from the chaplain, delivering the news that somebody done died. Feeling like you'd rather kill yourself than be handled like a wild fucking beast who no one gives a fuck about… And then, you wanna sit here and say you're sorry? Nigga, fuck being sorry. Ion want your fucking sorry, dog!"

Silent, Cateye was lost on words. Hearing his son's past few years burned a spot in his soul. He could never have imagined the suffering Michael went through and couldn't expect him to feel any less than how he already felt. He had every reason to.

"Micheal… I don't know what to say. Nothing I can say will change what happened. I only can ask that you try to forgive me for what I did." Cateye prayed within himself that he would in some way, even if it was only a little bit.

Whiteboy stared into his father's eyes, which were pleading for any form of forgiveness. Though he'd never be able to give it, not after all the shit he'd been through, including those things before prison. "I can't forgive neither of you." He stole a brief glance at his mother, then looked back at Cateye.

"Please, son, just at least try to find it in some part of your heart.

For us, Michael." So much emotion was emitting from Cateye. He seemed to be on the verge of crying, something Whiteboy had never seen him do before.

Whiteboy began to smile. He hadn't expected this but enjoyed every bit of it. "Sorry, but I buried my heart under the fucking prison."

Staring him in the face, Cateye saw this as a truism. No part of it was an act or fake. It was a reality check and one he was willing to accept. How could he refuse to when he'd participated as the creation?

"Cateye," Whiteboy wasn't finished, not even close, "it's only one reason I showed up here… and that was to be forgiven."

His father's lips became stilled. His mind was confused by the statement. Why would he be asking for forgiveness when he was the one wronged?

Whiteboy stood there a second, letting his words resonate, as well as allowing Cateye a moment – or two – to fully register what had been said, what had been truly meant, without having to be uttered.

Keeping eye to eye contact, Whiteboy's mind treaded upon the waters of the past, scratching the rippling surface of things and events he'd misunderstood and some he'd comprehended all too well. All of this was a mess because the more he stared, the more he saw a piece of him in his father's eyes – the more he saw that child, of a time ago, beg to be forgiven for actions he couldn't completely discern.

Inside, he somehow felt a new urge to pardon his parents for their transgressions, for every one of them. But he knew regardless of his feelings, he had to finish what had been started years ago. He had given himself his word that no matter what, it would be done once and for all.

I could never go back on my word, he reminded himself then quickly pulled out the snub nose .38 Bulldog.

Cateye gazed down at the black pistol, now understanding what really had rolled the rails of his son's mind for all these years. Whiteboy's mother became stiff at the sight of the gun, desperate to say something. Hell, anything capable of changing the current moment. She wished the impossible now, that time could rewind and undo all he'd been through and witnessed. Every struggle and misery he'd suffered since he'd been brought into this world.

Words continued to evade her while she attempted to maintain a smile. Tears began to ebb down her face.

"I love you..." she finally mumbled then turned to her husband, taking his hand in hers.

Cateye was still focused on the gun, mesmerized. He realized that he'd created the fate which found its way home for all the things they'd done to their child. He more than regretted it now.

Briefly, he looked into his wife's eyes then turned back to his son with two tears finding their way down his face. Whiteboy guessed they fell for the both of them. Judgement would be handed down by their own creation.

"I love you and..." the tears began to chase one another wildly with each word that left his mouth, "and I forgive you, son."

Whiteboy watched his parents as they both sobbed in unison, holding each other's hands, ready to leave together. The scene before his eyes actually seemed crazy to him. They'd been fully aware of how they'd treated him. How they'd put him through the most calamitous situations, which no regular child could have mentally made it through without ending up in some kind of asylum.

With that thought, Whiteboy continued to stand, gun down at his side. He stepped over the short space between him and them. His father glanced up at him as he came to a halt in front of him. Whiteboy glared at what had been the most detrimental factor of his life. However, at the moment, he somehow wished things were different – that Cateye would have chosen a different decision for them both.

Slowly, he raised the gun, aiming it directly at his forehead.

BOOM!!!

"Ah..." The sound had escaped his mother's lips. She couldn't believe that she'd just witnessed her husband's life exit out the back of his cranium. Her eyes turned to the muzzle that now made her its mark.

Whiteboy squeezed the trigger again, causing her body to slouch backwards like Cateye's had done.

He stood there, staring at the two lifeless shells of his parents. Whiteboy hoped they'd continue to be together in the afterlife.

"They deserve to..." he whispered under his breath. He began to smile upon seeing that their hands still clutched one another's.

Taking a step back, he viewed the silent house a second as the light aroma of blood and death began to settle into the atmosphere. Glancing up the hallway, he remembered something he'd always wanted and wondered if it was still in the same spot after all this time.

Whiteboy grinned, running quickly up the stairwell like he used to when he was younger.

"Fucking right!" he exclaimed, admiring the black .357 revolver that was accompanied with a pearl handle. It seemed wild that after all of the passing time, he'd find the gun exactly where he remembered it being, as if it was there waiting on him.

Stopping before leaving, he grabbed another glance at his parents. Walking over to where his father laid, he leaned over, kissing him on the forehead, right next to the bullet's entry point. "I forgive you," he said, hoping his words would be heard.

Whiteboy exited the house, leaving behind all the memories of the past. It was the perfect place for them to settle.

CHAPTER FOUR

"We trap or die, nigga…" Reno mumbled along with Young Jeezy's lyrics, patiently waiting to deliver information desired by the ones who'd become a steady part of his life.

At first, he would meet them once a week, but that quickly turned into three, sometimes four, times regardless of the time of day. The scheduling had become so irregular that he'd find himself exhausted from trying to manage tasks for them along with the ones Black was assigning to him, which was damn near every other minute.

Only a few more days, he thought, ready to finally end all it. Everything was going the way he wanted it to. In a couple of days, they'd pretend to buy from Black for the bust. Then, they would turn around and make a fake sale to Ace, knocking him out the box as well. That would leave all of the eastside up for grabs. Well, for anybody who possessed the money to conquer it.

Of course he didn't have the money. Though he was determined that if it was *anybody*, it was destined to be him. Especially, after he'd get the forty percent commission from both agents, White and Swift. They promised it once Ace and Black were both in the palms of their hands.

Ace though, probably wouldn't make his star appearance. Black was definitely in a hurry to be the cause of his demise. He had brought about the death of his right hand, Mal. *That shit was crazy*, he admitted to himself after bringing to mind the way Black had described how the people found him – broken up and chained to a tree with a few fingers missing. The scene had to be gruesome, which he knew was the reason for the closed casket funeral.

Mal had been the most loyal to Black, to the point of being stupid. *How the fuck did he let him persuade him into stepping in the center of death's circle?*

Reno had took heed to the occurrence, unlike the other soldiers who surrounded him. He realized it would only be a matter of time before he'd end up the exact same way if he continued to be Black's burden bearer, like he'd been so many times before. That was fo'sho a big no-no.

"Finally..." he uttered, watching the white SUV pull up beside his vehicle in the Burger King parking lot. He waited a moment before getting out of the Pontiac and quickly hopped in the backseat of the Ford.

"What's up?" greeted Reno, slamming the door. He peeked over the shoulder of the front seat in hopes of catching a sexy view of Ms. White.

"Hey." Agent White smiled lightly, craning her neck around. "So, how is everything coming along?" she questioned, jumping straight to business.

He sat back, loving her pretty face. "Shid, the shipment been put off for another two and a half weeks because of a few difficulties on the other end, but more or less, it's still a go. He just want to make sure y'all ready to cop, right?"

"How much he bringing in?" Swift asked blatantly, barging in on the conversation.

"Shhh…" Reno hated this muthafucka. "Ion know."

"Well, how about a damn estimation?"

"Shid…" Reno paused, trying to place a figure on Black's shit, which he knew would be wrong even if he made a million guesses.

Black had always been the secretive type, especially when it came down to business. Not even his closest associate knew his business, period, regardless of if it was funds or work.

"He mentioned that this would be his biggest shipment ever. So, I'm guessing about a couple hundred."

They both turned and eyed him curiously, kind of surprised.

"Hundreds of?" White insisted. Clearly, she had more than underestimated Black's net worth. For a while, they had put Black under surveillance and understood that he was supplying the entire eastside of Atlanta, including a few major parts of Fulton County and a few more small towns along the outskirts of the city. However, this information was astonishing.

"I think you already know." Reno chuckled at the expressions covering their faces.

"Wow..." White gasped, not believing it as she turned back around in her seat. She wondered if Swift was thinking the same thing she was. He had to be.

He glanced over at her and smiled. Surely this news was new music to their ears. It was an unexpected yet lovely melody, and they were more than grateful for it.

"Good fucking job!" Swift told him excitedly, unable to control his smile, joy – or whatever the hell you wanted to call it.

The words surprised Reno, causing him to feel a bit uncomfortable. It was unbelieving that those words had fallen from his mouth. The entire time they'd been meeting, never had Swift mouthed one good thing in his direction. It was always negative shit and threats, even when he'd done nothing to provoke such.

"Huh?" Reno still couldn't believe Swift's appreciation. He wanted to make sure he'd heard him correctly.

"GOOD-FUCKING-JOB!" He said it slowly this time with a laugh at the end, along with Agent White.

"Uh, aight..." was all Reno could manage, thinking that maybe he'd done a *good job* for real. *Maybe*, he thought, because it was only good from their perspective. In the streets, he'd be pictured as the most disgusting piece of shit that existed, which held the title of *rat*.

He somewhat cared about his persona in these streets, just not enough to put himself in the slammer with fifty some years.

Fuck that, he exclaimed to himself after exiting the SUV. He sat in his car, contemplating what his first move would be once all the eggs were in the basket. He'd been so caught up in his thoughts that he hadn't noticed the vehicle sitting across from him – the same one that had trailed him for over two weeks now.

"OH, D-NICE STUPID ASS FINALLY HERE," SAID ACE AS HIM AND Whiteboy parked in front of the spot. He saw that the kitchen light was on with one of his teammates pacing back-and-forth within it.

Heading toward the front door, he noticed everybody's whip except for Kero's. For some reason, this had become a usual, lately.

Making it to the door, he didn't even bother knocking. This was his territory, so he took the initiative and walked in after seeing the door was slightly cracked open. Most likely, they had seen him when he'd pulled up. But that still wouldn't make sense. One of the major rules had been the door was never to be unlocked. Ace firmly instilled that in his team.

"The fuck?" he grumbled right after pushing the door open. Ace stared a moment at the scene before him. Ariel was standing over D-nice, wrapping a bandage around his head as a blood-stained towel rested on his lap. To the left stood Dre, who displayed an expression that said, "You ain't gone like this."

D-nice's eyes fell directly on him when he first entered, but he waited a moment before getting Ariel's attention off the task at hand. She hadn't noticed that Ace stood only a few feet behind her.

"What? It hurt?" she asked, stopping midway around his cranium.

"The fuck going on?" questioned Ace, startling Ariel who spun in his direction a little too quickly.

"Hey..." She offered a halfhearted smile then glanced at D-nice like this was his cue to take center stage.

Ace heard Whiteboy shut the door as his mind ran over every

explanation which could possibly explain why Ariel was wrapping Nice's head up. What the fuck had he done?

"Nice, what the fuck going on?" he asked after shooting Dre a look. He left that to D-nice as well.

"B-bra…" he began, appearing as if he was searching for the right words. He found none. And not one time had he thought about how he would explain this to his big bro. "Bra, last night, some niggas ran down on me, and… and they hit *us* up." He struggled badly to let the last words fall from his lips.

"The fuck you mean?" Ace looked perplexed for a moment. The words hadn't registered yet. "Nigga, ex-fucking-plain."

"Last night, the power went out, and… and I went outside to see what happened and…" He paused, not really ready to fill him in on the rest. But Ace's stare told him that he didn't have a choice in the matter.

"Niggas came from nowhere. They snatched me up." His head dropped like he was a small child about to be reprimanded by his father. "They hit the spo…"

Ace began to move, snarling over his shoulder. "Nigga, hold up." Forcefully, he pushed the bathroom door open. He instantly caught sight of the wooden floor planks that remained out of place, the stash spot fully visible.

"Fuck!" he yelled, storming back into the living room. "Nigga…" Ace paused, glancing around. It didn't take long for him to notice that nothing else was out of place. Then, he looked in the rooms – where everything was still intact. He checked closely for anything unusual and out of place. Every part of the house was as he remembered it, except for the spot which held all their bread.

How? he had to ask himself, halting directly in front of D-nice.

"Shawty…" Glaring down at him, Ace snatched the Ruger from his waistline. "D… bra, I know you not trying to fucking play me. How the fuck some niggas look over every fucking thing else in this bitch, except for the muthafucking spot?"

D-nice sat there in total silence. A scared silence. Damn, he had fucked up. Now, what was he supposed to tell Ace? That he told them while dude was holding the strap to his head? "Bra, they had me down bad."

Ace snapped. "Nigga, fuck that. Where the fuck is my shit at?" He aimed the pistol at D-nice's head now.

"Ace, my nigga, you think I had some'n to do with it?" D-nice's expression said that Ace had just stuck the knife in his heart.

"Nigga, explain it. You was here – by yourself. You took your dumb ass outside when you already know the no-leaving-the-spot rule. But you still did it. Now, you saying some niggas ran down on you then went straight to the stash spot – a spot that only *we* knew about. D-nice, tell me what the fuck else am I pose to think?"

Everybody in the room laid their eyes on D-nice. Ace had made a point. Ariel and Dre hadn't even paid attention to the house since they'd been in it. Their focus the entire time had been on D-nice's wound, which Ace clearly didn't care about.

"Tell me how they missed the entire fucking house, except for the fucking spot? And ain't asking you again."

D-nice realized he had no other choice now. He would either tell him or die by way of seeming guilty. He hesitated a moment, staring at them all before dropping his head. "I told them..." He uttered it a tad higher than a whisper.

"What?" Ace growled, thinking – rather wishing – that he'd heard him wrong.

"I told 'em..." he repeated louder.

"Bitc..." Ace jumped at him, on the verge of hitting him with the pistol. But Ariel quickly wrapped her arms around his waist, stopping him only mere inches away from completing his objective.

"Bae... bae, chill," she encouraged, hoping to calm him.

"Man, fuck that! This nigga done," he snarled, pushing her hands away.

"White..." she called out, still trying to keep hold of him.

In unison, Whiteboy and Dre aided her in trying to restrain him from going ape shit on his intended victim.

"Ace, chill, bra. Chill," Dre coached. Yet he really wanted to let him dish out what Nice deserved. Shid, he had put all of them in a fucked-up position. However, Dre hated he had to see that look in Ariel's eyes. Had it not been for her, shit would have been over.

"Man, watch out!" growled Ace, pushing off of them, taking a few regretful steps backwards. "Fuck this nigga… Fuck ass nigga you gave my shit away – all because you got caught witcha fucking draws down… Pussy ass nig…" He couldn't even finish his sentence. Ace was way too angry to.

Glaring at him, Ace thought of a thousand things he would take pleasure in doing to him. Sure, he probably would be wrong, but shid, he'd be able to live with it. D-nice had majorly fucked-up – and over – the entire team.

Ace continued to stare at him menacingly. *How could he be so stupid? So fucking gullible?* The D-nice he'd known wouldn't have gone for that bullshit. They would have had to show him first. Couldn't no muthafuckas instill enough fear in him to make him do anything. But this seemed to be the case.

It was unrealistic. How could a nigga just hand over three hundred and fifty thousand?

Ace shook his cranium, not believing it. Though he knew that if pressure was applied righteously, even the toughest niggas could be broken as well.

But why was this understanding coming with at a six-figure cost? He didn't want to accept it – couldn't – especially facing their current situation with Black. They couldn't afford it. Definitely not now.

Look at this fucking coward, he thought. Still pacing back-and-forth, Ace stared threateningly. The urge to kill him was very present. He more than understood that he had to get him out of his face, or he would.

"Shawty, get the fuck out!"

D-nice, along with everyone else in the room, turned their gaze toward him. Their expressions were a mix of confusion and surprise. None of them had anticipated this. And as the realization dawned on D-nice, he knew he had fucked up bad. His actions settled heavily upon him, though he couldn't fathom the extent of Ace's reaction. He was being casted out from the only place he truly considered home, a title this place earned through time.

Now, what am I supposed to do? D-nice began to think, sitting motionless – speechless – and unable to prevent his gaze from sweeping over the only family he had known – the only family he wanted.

"Bra—" was the only word D-nice's trembling lips could get out before he was cut off.

"Man, fuck that. Get-the-fuck-out! Ain't shit to talk about unless it's this muthafucking pistol," he snapped, lifting the gun again for his eyes to see. Then, he snatched the front door open.

"Ace, don't…" Ariel uttered with intentions of her words being interpreted as a plea.

He shook his head harder, not wanting to hear any of that. "Nah, fuck that! Ain't no room on this muthafucking team for cowards."

With that, nothing was to – or would – be said in his defense. His fate had been decided.

They all watched as D-nice hung his head low before treading beyond the threshold he'd probably never enter again.

Ace slammed the door hard enough to make the walls shake. Instantly, he became very annoyed by all the eyes on him.

"What?" he snapped, compelling them all to advert their gazes. Well, all besides Ariel.

She crossed her arms, giving him that look, which always let him know when he was in the wrong. He hated it. Usually, he'd take heed to the cold stare, or at least attempt to correct whatever harm he'd caused. Not today though. He wouldn't, no matter how long she bored into him with those eyes. Today was different – a three hundred-and-fifty-thousand-dollar difference.

"So?" Whiteboy said inquisitively, caring less about the occurrence. He was ready to map out the solution.

Ace had heard him. Yet he chose to ignore him, along with Ariel's expression, as he moved past them both for the refrigerator. After taking a long drag from a Tropicana orange juice, which he briefly pretended to inspect, his eyes found their way to Whiteboy, who displayed a sinister grin.

"Shid..." Ace tried to return the same exact grin. "My shit got fucked up, so you know it's a must Black shit get fucked up too." It wasn't at all hard for him to lay the blame at Black's feet.

"WE BOUT TO TEAR THIS NIGGA ASS UP," GRUMBLED ONE OF BLACK'S soldiers, who was being led by Pee Pee in the assault on Ace.

Pee Pee sat in the front, clutching onto the AR-15, more than ready to let it do Black's work. To everyone else a part of this small hit squad, this had been just another command by Black to prove their loyalty. But to him, it would be his moment of stardom, which he'd longed for for so many months.

Since the first time him and Ace had met, he wanted badly to end him for all the times he'd dissed him in front of Black – all the times he'd belittled him as nothing more than a mere peon, who only begged for a chance to be the top nigga on Black's dick while he stood at the pinnacle of Black's veneration.

To Pee Pee, Ace was Black's golden knight, the son he always held in high esteem until recently. At first, he couldn't understand why his chief in command put up with Ace's disrespectful ways. He thought that it was just the way their father-son relationship went until Black had finally relayed the story of Ace.

Damn, was the only remark Pee Pee could think of after listening to what seemed like the rough draft of a movie script. A script which added more fuel to the fire of his envy, especially after finding out that little Ace was of no *real* relation to Black. He was just another young nigga kicked to the streets with nothing and no one – exactly how he had been.

Ace was different though. He'd set the standard in Black's eyes that every nigga after him tried to exceed but always ended up short when it was all said and done. In a sense, he remained the one Black subliminally told them to admire – the one he wanted all of them to imitate.

Pee Pee was jealous of the spotlight that Ace had rightfully deserved, and he became determined to step in and conquer it, removing the *one* who was ungrateful to the hand that had created him. The one who was the real reason for that spotlight even existing.

Now, the time had come for him to show that he was capable of being vicious, fierce, and a loyalist – the new favorite. Tonight, he would prove he'd been destined for such a place within the circle of beasts. Tonight, he would kill the feared and untouched shining knight.

"Aye, where we need to turn at?" the driver asked, bringing Pee Pee out of his reverie of glory.

"Go down to the second street then make a right," he said, pointing down the dark street.

Making the necessary turn, the van crept along the street, exactly like Pee Pee instructed. He'd been here a few times, so he knew they were only a short distance away from their target.

"Lock and load," he said over his shoulder, barely craning his neck as he launched a round into the chamber.

Approaching, Pee Pee could see a few shadowed figures stepping out onto the yard. *Perfect,* he wanted to say, eyeing the situation as if it were designed by fate itself.

"Pull over… pull over," whispered Pee Pee, slightly opening the van's door mere yards away from the two of them. He could hear the rear door slide backwards as he slid out, ducking low. He wanted to creep up on his prey.

BOOM!!! BOOM!!!

Gun shots suddenly erupted. The figures had fired at them first. Obviously, they'd peeped the move before they could own the advantage.

Pee Pee lifted the assault rifle face level and began to squeeze the trigger with a purpose, aiming into the night.

The shootout ensued from both sides. It was like the turf had instantly transformed into Desert Storm.

Pee Pee lurched forward fearlessly with the rest of his fellow comrades following suit, unloading on the whole scene before them.

"Fuck! I'm hit." He heard someone scream out from somewhere on the side. Continuing to man the rifle recklessly, he turned his head to see who was down. It was Cap, one of the dudes Black had used a few times before. But he was also one he could afford to lose as a casualty for the sake of completing the task at hand.

As soon as his eyes set back on the direction he'd been shooting at, he quickly caught a glimpse of flashes coming from behind a vehicle which sat at the house next door. Unhesitatingly, he took aim and fired.

The clock was ticking on the inside of his head. It was time to go. And if his internal timer hadn't been enough, then the police sirens wailing streets away were certainly the signal to haul ass.

Retreating backwards, he continued to shoot, hoping that they'd at least downed an arm of the opposition in case they hadn't lucked up and killed the head.

"Aye, aye!" he yelled at the rest of them that were making their way onto the edge of the lawn. Immediately, they stopped firing as if they understood without him having to utter another word.

As they sprinted toward the van that was moving in their direction, Pee Pee glanced over at Cap, who laid in the street begging for one of them to help.

"Pee Pee... Bra, hel-help me," he groaned out in pain as blood spewed from the corners of his mouth.

Pee Pee only stared down at him. Then, Black's words resonated throughout his mental. *No room for the injured.* He aimed the rifle, quickly letting two rounds cease the life of his fallen comrade.

Hopefully along with a life on the other side, he thought as they pulled away from the scene.

<hr>

CHAPTER FIVE

<hr>

"Well, damn, no war back?" chuckled Black. He inhaled the Kush smoke, thinking about the card he'd dealt Ace and how there was nothing of an after effect, which had been unusual for his former apprentice.

Upon hearing the details of the short shootout, he was certain that they hadn't killed Ace. But now as the days passed, he began to doubt his first mind. Especially realizing that none of the people who he'd set up in parts of East Atlanta had mentioned one single sighting of him or his crew.

Maybe he'd gotten the point. And if he hadn't and wasn't touched by the first attempt on his life, Black's gunmen would continue to send bullets his way until one met its mark.

Black wanted to laugh. Never had he imagined that he'd witness a day when Ace would retreat after just one swift gun battle. In fact, to be blunt, he had anticipated multiple casualties from the brief run in with the expectation that Ace would at least be injured in the process. They would have been sacrifices Black was willing to make and which would be made if that was what it took to clear the path for the final blow. He had determined that it was time to remove Ace from the picture permanently.

At the moment though, it seemed like he had accomplished what he thought would be a couple month's task in one night.

Impossible. He smiled, dumping ashes from the blunt. Black took another pull before handing it to his newfound captain, Pee Pee. He studied him closely, watching him inhale the smoke. Black began to contemplate as to whether or not he could stand up to the position he now held.

In his honest opinion, Pee Pee didn't possess the necessary characteristics of the position's predecessor, Mal. But he did walk around with the heart of three of him, minus the emotional attachments. Pee Pee, he often noticed, was bold when the time called for it. He was just too damn talkative and friendly. A socialite would best describe him – until you made him mad, something he'd witnessed firsthand. The young boy carried a mean temper.

Ever since that day, Black knew he had a natural on his hands whose sole flaw was being a people's person. Though over a period of time, Black would come to understand that was just the way he was. And he accepted it, but he needed to make him into a mixture of both Ace and Mal. Half... sporadic. The other half, strategic. Yet both extremely deadly.

"So, what's the move?" Pee Pee finally asked, releasing the acrid smoke toward the room's ceiling.

"You already know what we waiting on," Black responded, analyzing the blunt before speaking again. "The muthafucking blessing from Heaven itself." He chuckled along with Pee Pee because his statement was true in every sense. Tomorrow, Black would be hit with a shitload of blow. It was enough to supply the entire state – well, more than half like he intended to.

The reason for the two-week delay had been the Ace situation. In his eyes, Ace was an actual *threat* to the business opportunity at hand, and there was no way in hell he'd let him fuck it up. Period. He knew

Ace would be willing to do anything to wreck his plans and definitely after having knowledge of it, courtesy of himself.

At first, all he wanted to do was include him in on a *once in a life-time* profitable business venture, a thing beneficial for both of them. Ace would rack up numbers he'd never imagined.

This – in Black's mind – held the potential of healing the deep wound which had gushed forth more bad blood between the two of them. Black – since he could remember – had never cared for any nigga. Yet with Ace, his feelings were different. To him, Ace was the son he never had – the little brother he always wanted to guide and be a role model to.

When he first took him in, Ace was just another young nigga who he would selfishly use at his own disposal. However, as time passed, Ace grew on him, something that seemed odd to Black at the time. Never had he let anyone close enough to actually make him feel any type of way when it came down to this street shit. Ace, though, had accomplished that.

He had become to Black what a cub was to a lion – a child to protect and, on the same token, one to teach its very own survival skills.

However, that was then, before the bond was broken. Before the Mal shit – before the skeletons fell out of the closet.

Now, the damage was beyond repair, and they were opposing forces.

Two weeks and some days had passed, and still there was no Ace. His continuing absence would be great for business, even if it was more than temporary. But Black wouldn't be naïve. Ace – he was certain – would come, and he'd be waiting.

"Pee…" Black began, dubbing out the last of the blunt. "Tomorrow, I want niggas all the way on point. I don't need nobody – I mean no-fuck-ing-body – slipping. A nigga can't afford a fuck up on this shit. Too much on the line. If a nigga fuck this up," he paused, stepping close to be face-to-face with Pee Pee, "he dies wit the fuck-up being his last regret. No-fucking-exceptions!" he finished, emphasizing with a snap of his fingers.

Pee Pee stared at him seriously, understanding the importance of the situation and his concern. "I got you, big dawg." His state of mind tomorrow would be like the army going into World War II. Every "T" would be crossed and every "I" dotted. Anything besides maneuvering toward victory wouldn't be accepted.

Ain't no fucking way, Pee Pee said to himself as Black began to lay out the details of tomorrow's activities.

"GIRL, I NEEDED THIS..." LATOYA SMILED EXUBERANTLY, ENJOYING the little vacation which Sassy had, out of the blue, insisted on. She'd gotten the call from her best friend, who sounded distraught – babbling so quickly that she almost didn't catch a word she said.

"Slow down, girl. What's wrong?" Latoya had asked, but Sassy ignored her question. Then the words every girl could understand, no matter how distorted they were, came through the phone. "It's on me... South Beach."

Those few words caused her to forget about the strange sound riding her friends voice. Free and in South Beach would cause any female to lose track of thought – or concern for their friend.

They had met up at the nail salon in Atlanta Station. Sassy had run down only a few things that had taken place between her and the love of her life. She sounded awkward trying to explain half of the reason why she'd been in such urgent need for the trip.

Two hours later after getting a rental car, they were on I-75 riding to the tunes of Beyoncé, talking about everything that came to mind. Latoya had preferred to take a plane, so Sassy had to show her why they couldn't.

"Now girl why is you taking that?" Latoya inquired after Sassy revealed the handgun to her.

"Bitch, all these crazy ass people out here. My pregnant ass a rather be safe than sorry." Sassy said, hoping the statement would be enough. There was no way she could explain why Ace whole heartedly insisted that she take it as a *precaution*.

. . .

Now the sun rays gleamed on their skin as they idly wandered along the beach's sand, verbalizing their usual girl talk. The atmosphere was very unique, full of fresh air and life. Everyone they treaded past appeared to radiate elation and was quite obviously accustomed to strutting around barely clothed while enjoying the evening's breeze as the sun set. The aroma of exotic sexual hormones and alcohol touched every sensation spot within their nostrils.

"You ain't the only one..." Sassy giggled, letting the relaxing sound of the waves sooth her mental. Mountains of stress and worry had clouded her horizon since the morning of her and Ace's disagreement. She couldn't understand it. Out of all the mishaps he'd had in relation to the streets, there was never an *occurrence* which became so serious that he'd felt as though his family would be endangered. This was new, and it scared her more and more with each passing hour.

What happened? She was dying on the inside to know. When Ace was at home, the streets were left with the streets. She always respected the fact that he refused to even mention the littlest of events which took place in that world. At home, it was about him, her, and their world. Regardless of what time of the day it would be, that part would always be her favorite of the day.

Her thoughts drifted back to that morning with her standing in the hallway. Sassy couldn't believe her eyes. She stood there witnessing a part of the man she loved, which she'd never seen before. The fierce tone riding in his voice aroused her some – she had to admit – yet not as much as it scared her.

Standing in awe, she tried her best to listen while he continued snapping into the phone. She wondered who was on the other end and what *bitch* would be the death of somebody. And what had Ace done to Mal?

His words caused so much confusion within her brain that she didn't know whether to ask or not, but she had to be her. She asked, and he ignored. Sassy, being Sassy, probed on, which unexpectedly caused him – she later understood – to grab her with an expression on his face that said *something* other than Ace was present at the moment. His grip tightened, and she couldn't help but to stare at the demonically possessed person in front of her. A person the streets had created and feared, she knew.

Quickly, she became frightened, though not for her own safety but for the safety and wellbeing of the person she loved the most. It was Ace and Ace only that made every day worth another breath. He'd been her world since the first time she laid eyes on him. He was her Ace.

When he first told her that she had to leave what she cared about, she cried. She didn't want to but knew he wouldn't have it any other way besides his own. How could she just leave and have to bear thoughts of him being injured or worst – gone? Once, she'd told him sincerely that if he was to die, she would rather die along with him. To her, everything which existed in her world lied within every part of him. He had chuckled at the words, touching her stomach, before replying, "This is *our* world."

The memory almost brought tears to her eyes while she continued to lay tracks in the sand next to Latoya's. The setting was a little too perfect for tears right now.

"So, girl, how we gone do this tonight? The club or theeee ccclluuubbb!?" Latoya laughed, showing a little too much excitement.

"The club? With all this?" Sassy questioned with furrowed eyebrows, rubbing her stomach. Their world.

Latoya sucked her teeth. "Girl, I done seen plenty of pregnant bitches in the club."

"Yeah, ratchet bitches," Sassy reminded her.

"I don't give a fuck bitches." Latoya laughed.

This was one of the reasons she'd been Sassy's only friend. She always knew how to make the best out of an otherwise ugly situation. She always knew what it took to make her laugh, while still keeping it real, unlike regular females in the city.

Sassy shook her head at the thought of being in that type of environment, carrying six and a half months of luggage. Ace would kill her – and Latoya – if he found out that they were only standing next to the building.

"Okay, Latoya..." Sassy finally spoke, placing both hands on her hips. "What can I possibly do with all this?"

Latoya twisted her lips a little, as if giving her *restriction* some real thought. Not many things came to mind. "Maybeee we can just go somewhere nice for a few drinks. I mean, I don't think that would hurt," she finished, her face contorted into that of a child begging Mommy to go to Six Flags.

Sassy hated when she did this and couldn't help but to give in to her desperateness. Hell, what girl wanted to be in Miami and not experience the best it had to offer?

"Now, where exactly are we going to have those drinks?" Sassy questioned curiously.

Before Latoya could respond, Sassy noticed a brown-skinned male. He had the body of a fitness trainer with braids trailing down to his shoulders. His movement made it seem like he was heading in their direction. And his Colgate smile assured her that they were his intended destination. However, none of that was what actually caught her attention. The fact that he seemed, for some odd reason, familiar was what adverted her gaze from her friend.

Latoya quickly recognized Sassy's change of expression. Instantly, she pivoted toward the direction of her friend's curiosity. As soon as she did, a handsome, fine ass man rocking a wife beater and Louis Vuitton flip flops was pacing only a few feet away from them and coming.

My God! she thought, giving his physique another thorough inspection.

"How are you ladies this evening?" he mouthed smoothly with his mellow tone. He extended a hand.

"Fine and you?" Latoya greeted him with the sexiest voice she could muster, taking the initiative to speak for both of them.

Sassy said nothing, only looked at him suspiciously. She was still trying to put her finger on whether or not she'd really seen him before. If so, where? And if not, why did she feel so convinced that she had?

Sassy wasn't the type to pay attention to men, especially not to the extent that she'd actually remember them, but this nigga would make a bitch, at least, have a second glance and thought. He was definitely fine, just not as fine as her Ace, which was the only dude, man, and nigga she ever thought about.

So, why was she still feeling that, somehow, she'd come across him somewhere before? And it wasn't in South Beach. *Maybe he just got some similar features of someone I seen*, she began to think. Then again, the way he stared at her as he approached…

"Sassy..." Latoya uttered, bringing her from the brief daydream with a slight nudge of the elbow.

"Oh… hey," she said nonchalantly, refusing to acknowledge his extended hand toward her.

He smiled. "My name's Prince."

Before he had the chance to say anything else, Latoya blurted out, "I'm Latoya, and this is my pregnant, *married* best friend, Sassy."

Sassy shot her an inquisitive glance. Yes, anybody could see that she was pregnant but married? At least not yet, though she caught her drift.

"As I can see..." he returned with a slight chuckle, giving her stomach a second glance.

The way he looked at her made it seem as if he knew her, like his mind was taunting her, saying, "Uh, you don't remember me.'"

A shiver went down her spine.

"I was wondering," he smiled, putting his attention back on Latoya, "if I could treat you nice ladies to a few drinks and hopefully be granted a chance to know y'all, if," he swept his gaze to Sassy briefly, "that isn't too much to ask."

"That's crazy because me and my friend…" Latoya gleefully hooked one of Sassy's arms with hers, giving her a *be good* look, "we was just thinking of having a few *drinks* ourselves."

"Oh, where were y'all planning on going?" he asked, very interested.

"Well, nowhere really. We don't know of any of the places down here."

"Okay, in that case, let me treat both of *you* to one of the best lounges down here."

"And that's?" Latoya inquired, really not caring. She just wanted to seem a bit classy. He could have taken her to the moon for all she cared.

"The Bleau Bar..."

"The Bleau Bar? Sounds... kinda low grade," said Sassy, studying him carefully. She began to wonder why he hadn't bothered to ask where they were from. That was usually a guy's next question, but it wasn't his when Latoya had clearly indicated – quite simply – that they weren't from around here.

He gave her that smile again.

"Girl, the Bleau Bar is one of the classiest spots on the entire South Beach strip. But I'm glad to see you won't go for anything," he said with a small chuckle.

"Don't mind my friend. She's like, you know, the anti-social type," Latoya apologized. She could see where this was about to go if she continued to let Sassy direct the conversation. There was no way she'd miss out on having drinks with Mr. Fine.

"No, I'm not," Sassy let out, giving Latoya a look, then turned back to him. "I just really believe in Drake's words. Uh, you know the song, *No New Friends?*"

He laughed as if to say, *That was a good one.* "I feel you, Ma, but I'm not trying to be a *friend*. Just looking for a nice time with some beautiful strangers for a while."

Before Sassy could respond, Latoya thought better of it and beat her to the punch. "And you have found the beautifulest two."

Sassy twisted her lips at Latoya's remark. *Why is she so thirsty?*

"I see. Well, what time will you ladies be free?"

"Let's say... round about..." Latoya glanced down at her Micheal Kors' watch. "Bout nine thirty. Give us a lil time to freshen up."

"Perfect. And what hotel is y'all staying at?"

"Why?" Sassy asked skeptically.

"Girl, ch..." Latoya didn't get a chance to finish.

"How else am I going to know where to scoop y'all, Ms. Meanie?" he returned, grinning.

"You don't have to worry about that. We got our own car," Sassy said in a way that wasn't meant to be delightful.

"Cool, so what's the number?"

"I'll give you mine..." Latoya insisted, shooting Sassy a fake smile, the same one she always gave whenever they were in front of company. This was her way of letting her know they were going to have words afterwards.

Sassy stood there watching the two exchange numbers with a few words of small talk. She turned, gazing at the beautiful horizon. The sun's rays skimmed across the surface of the ocean. The current of the water splashed over the top of her feet. Man, she wished Ace was here, holding her as they watched this lovely view. The mood would be intimate and perfect – spectacular in every aspect. The only word she thought of was empyrean.

"So, that was all about?" Latoya asked, breaking Sassy free from the impeccable reverie.

"What?" she returned, glancing over her shoulder at the guy named Prince, who was walking away.

"What you mean, what? Why was you acting so... so you?" Latoya laughed a bit.

"Toya, it's something about him."

"I know that's right..." Latoya joked, pushing her on the shoulder slightly.

"No, for real. I don't like his vibe."

"Sassy, who vibe do you *like* besides Ace? And well, mines?"

"Not you... just Ace," Sassy returned jokingly. "But I can't put my finger on it. It's like I've seen him somewhere before. I don't know and the way he looked at me. It was like he knew I knew him or something."

"Sassy, girl, listen to yourself. Don't you think if he would of even thought that y'all knew each other in any type of way, he would of gladly said so?"

Sassy understood her point, but there still existed a feeling deep within her which said otherwise. "Yeah, I guess. But alright, why didn't…" She cut her own words short, realizing that if she continued to carry on, it would only sound more berserk to her friend's ears. She decided to let it go. "Never mind. So, what you want to get into now?"

"Girl, I thought you would never ask. I got just the thing."

"Oh, Lord. I wonder what that is." Sassy smiled because she knew whatever Latoya had in mind would be crazy but fun nonetheless.

CHAPTER SIX

"Agh!!!" Mal screened out as he sat tied in the chair. Ace twisted the grip pliers, which were clamped down on Mal's big toe.

"Nigga, the spot in Kirkwood," Ace snarled. He loosened up a little on the pressure.

"Ace, ma-man, I told you, bra..." He groaned in pain.

"Nigga, yo bitch ass ain't told me shit!" Ace snapped, beginning to twist them again, this time with a vengeance.

"No! No, bra... Agh!" Mal whimpered.

Ace smiled in satisfaction. "Tell me now, muthafucka."

"Ace..." he mumbled through hard breaths. "Man, the shit in the wall... behi-behind the refrigerator."

Ace smiled, remembering how he'd completely broken the notorious Mal literally as he sat in the driver's seat of the Infinity SUV. He was directly across from the spot he'd told him about.

Ace was ready to send a message to Black for the little bullshit stunt he pulled by sending his fake ass hit squad at them. It had been two weeks and a half since the incident occurred. Him and Whiteboy were walking toward the Benz when he spotted the van creeping its way down the street.

Ace wanted to laugh, wondering what type of stupid shit they were trying to pull, but he would quickly find out. The shooters had sprung from it blasting – but only after he'd taken the initiative in letting off the first round. The gun fight left his whip, Ariel's Lexus, Dre's Escalade, and the spot with a multitude of bullet holes and one other exception – his very own shoulder being grazed by one.

That shit hurt like hell, he recalled. Although that would be nothing compared to the havoc he planned on unleashing on his adversary and his entourage.

Now, here he was. about to deliver the first blow of his payback.

His eyes scrutinized the apartment meticulously while he waited patiently in the night. He was accompanied by Whiteboy, Dre, and Kero. The small apartments sat right around the corner from the hood they were all from, so the location was all too familiar.

When Mal first made mention of it, Ace figured he'd been misleading them until one night, he decided to investigate, whereas he witnessed a good bit of *strange* traffic to and from the apartment. If he didn't know anything, he knew the signs of a trap spot. And all the indicators of one were present and wouldn't have been seen if he'd just been an average muthafucka.

Tonight was the eighth night he'd laid on it. And it would be the night he got some of his due reparations.

"Man, who we waiting on, bra? Jesus?" Kero asked from the backseat, impatient as always.

"Bra, chill..." responded Ace, glancing down at his phone to check the time. It wouldn't be too much longer.

Ever since he began surveillance of the place, he noticed that at two thirty, a dark blue BMW X One would drive up with a dude going into the apartment. He'd stay for like fifteen minutes tops then come back out. Every single time, he'd have a duffle bag in tow – exactly like Mal had told him.

It was two twenty-five.

"Say..." began Ace. His gaze remained locked on the target until his phone vibrated. *The fuck she want at this time of night?* he thought after glancing at the number. Whatever it was, the shit would have to wait.

Ignoring the call, he got back to what he was about to say. "Y'all already know what's what when y'all see me move." With those words, Ace stealthily eased out of the driver's seat.

Ducking low, he moved across the lot, coming to a stop on the side of a parked vehicle. He was out of sight of the apartment's front window and any set of eyes that just so happen to pop up onto the scene unexpectedly.

He dropped into a crouched position and waited on his prey. Ace listened tentatively for any sounds of acceleration. He was very aware that at the entrance of the apartments stood a steep hill that would cause any motor to roar climbing it. That would be his cue.

"Damn," he huffed to himself, finding it a bit difficult to keep the crouched position. First, he attempted to stay in a squat, but that quickly put a strain on his thighs. Then, he dropped to one knee, but the concrete wouldn't allow that for too long either. So now, he straightened his legs, bending at the waist, deciding that when the time came, he'd resume his crouched posture. *It shouldn't be long.*

He was just about to glance at his time piece until he heard that loud resonating sound he'd been waiting on. Peeking around the rear end of the car, he watched the bright headlights of a vehicle illuminate the entire scenery. This made it hard for him to make out the type of vehicle it was, but once it swerved into the parking space opposite of him, a brief side view let him know that the target had arrived.

Like clockwork, he thought, snatching back the slide of the nine-millimeter Beretta. Stealthily, he inched his way around the car, coming to a stop at the rear. He saw good reasoning in allowing whoever it was in the X One some time to get out. There was no way he would run up on the whip with the door still closed. That would be a rookie move in his opinion and one which could end up fatal.

Click.

The door opened with the individual taking a step onto the asphalt. Before his other foot had the chance to do the same, Ace was up on him, shoving the pistol into the side of his face while gripping the collar of his button down.

"Man…" the guy had the intentions of saying something, but Ace quickly silenced him.

"Nigga any sound, I'ma down you." He paused briefly a second to let the statement sink into his skull like the bullet would if he chose otherwise.

The dude's expression went from being one of shock to that of being overly terrified. A pistol touching the side of your jaw had a way of having that effect.

"Nigga, we going to the door, and you gonna get me in. Anything besides that, I burn you and whoever on the other side, feel me?" Ace snarled with an expression denoting he'd make good of every word.

The guy nodded in understanding. Ace still decided to watch him closely. This was seeming to be all too easy, especially for the caliber of niggas Black used within the Hand.

"Aight, let's do it…" Letting him step out, Ace quickly frisked the guy's waistline for anything that would motivate him to do something dumb. After the brief search, he took a step backwards, giving dude some room to move from the small space between the SUV and its open door, yet he kept the Beretta against his face.

"Remember…" Ace spoke lowly, tapping the strap against his skull as a reminder while they proceeded toward the front door of both of their reasons for being here tonight.

As they stepped closer, Ace could hear light, small footsteps quickly closing in on his rear. He didn't have to turn around. They were his squad.

Walking through the doorway of the corridor, Ace ducked low, putting his back against the wall, keeping the pistol steady on its target, while Whiteboy and the rest of them stood on the stairs right outside.

Dude knocked three times then just stood there, switching his eyes between the door and Ace, a little too rapidly.

"Nigga…" Ace lowly growled through clenched teeth, shaking his head.

"Yo, yo." He heard someone shout from the inside. The guy didn't respond until Ace shoved the pistol toward his crotch, aided by an almost inaudible mumble of, "Keep playing."

He stood there, shaking a little, staring at the door as the individual repeated. "Yo, yo."

Finally, he replied. "More or less, just us."

Ace could see that Black had gotten smart and implemented a little code system amongst his band of soldiers. He wasn't sure if the phrase would be for the better or worse, but nonetheless, as soon as dude uttered it, the locks began to click.

Ace deviously smirked up at the dude and speedily came off the wall, maneuvering into an angle where he'd have the advantage once the door opened. The door shook then went ajar.

The guy, who he'd ran down on, pivoted quickly around as the door spread wider, reaching for Ace's gun.

"Nig…" Ace yelped, pushing him and at the same time pulling the trigger. The blast echoed throughout the hallway. Ace fired again, pushing the dude towards the apartment's interior. Ace forced his entire body to crash into the floor after the door gave way. The other guy scrambled out of the way with his hand fidgeting at his waistline.

Hastily snatching his gun from the dude's grasp, he swung it upward, shooting the inside guy twice while he continued struggle with the first dude.

Stepping over the one under him, Ace moved for the other guy, whose hand continued to fiddle for the weapon that was obviously stuck. He locked his aim on him while he squirmed like a wounded animal.

"Don't, nigga," he told him, bending over, pressing the muzzle in the center of his forehead, removing what he'd been unsuccessful at.

Damn, Ace thought, knowing they didn't have much time now. Anybody who was in the complex at this moment had certainly heard the gunshots, which meant a phone call to the police was quite possibly being placed. Time was definitely of the essence.

"Bitch ass nigga," grumbled Whiteboy, smacking the first guy Ace had shot in the face with the butt of his gun.

"Fuc…" he let out. His hands were pressed against the holes in his torso as if they were trying to plug the leaks.

"Nigga…" Ace kicked him in the side. "Where that shit at?" He was glad to see that Dre, along with Kero, weren't wasting time splitting past him, heading for the back rooms.

"Nigga, ion know… what th-fuc you… talking bou…" he spit out through sharp breaths, trying to roll onto his side.

Ace stopped him midway. "Bet." With that, he planted a round into his skull. Initially, he'd hoped that there existed something Mal failed to mention. Yet he couldn't afford to waste time dealing with the *tell me or I'll kill you* game.

Moving from the lifeless, he tucked both of the pistols down into his pants while the sounds of Whiteboy continuing to pistol whip dude mercilessly rang out.

Fuck it. Ace smirked, thinking he deserved it for the dumb attempt he'd pulled. He stood in front of the refrigerator, grateful for his former mentor's knowledge. He'd told him that his pot of gold laid just beyond this small obstacle.

"Say…" he yelled loud enough, causing not only Whiteboy but Dre and Kero to appear in the kitchen's doorway.

Reluctantly, Whiteboy released the shirt of the battered man, letting him – unconsciously – slump to the floor. He walked into the kitchen, gazing down at the bloodied pistol, smiling at the fact that he'd gone overboard.

Ace began feeling for some leverage, slightly leaning over the cabinet, now realizing he would have to pull it out a bit so Whiteboy could help by pulling from the other side. If he failed to, White wouldn't be able to aid him because of a wall which blocked the other side.

At first, it didn't budge, whereupon he forced his hip against the cabinet and tugged harder. It inched forward a little, stopping because Whiteboy pressed his foot against the bottom. Gripping the top, he yanked it toward himself before Ace even had a chance to stop him.

The refrigerator tilted forward, making both of them clear its way as it fell to the floor. The open space behind it was now fully exposed.

"Bingo!" said Ace, ready to see what laid inside. Hopping on the fridge's back, he took a quick peek at the treasure within. The hole was dark as hell, to the point that even with the kitchen light being on, he still couldn't tell what was in it. But nonetheless, he could tell that something was bulging in the darkness.

Reaching in with his right arm, he used his left one to prevent himself from falling into the orifice. Instantly, his hand felt some type of clothed bag. Snatching it, he brought it from the mouth of the wall. Ace almost sneezed as a cloud of dust raced into his face. Quickly, he tossed the tote bag to Whiteboy then reached back in for whatever he could feel next.

Fuck, he thought as his hand roamed around the inside. Nothing. He refused to believe it was only one duffle.

"Fuck it..." he huffed, beginning to get irritated. "Let's dip." He mouthed it loud enough for all three of them to hear.

Ace hoped like hell Dre and Kero had found something valuable because there was no way he went through all the trouble for one fucking duffle bag.

Upon seeing them, his gaze dropped instinctively to their hands. Nothing. *Man, what the fuck?!* he shouted inside of his head while letting the trio exit first. He looked down at the battered man, who continued to emit sounds from the depths of his throat. Ace guessed he was gargling on his own blood.

Smirking and satisfied at the job Whiteboy had done, Ace pulled the strap out and took aim, firing two rounds into the man's face. He then let the gun collide with the wooden floor as he stepped over the body and backed out into the hallway.

Moving with more momentum, Ace leaped down the five steps, snatching the door handle to the X One, which still had the keys in the ignition. Hopefully, they'd find more once the BMW was searched, he thought as he reversed and began tailing White and them.

Sitting at the table, they looked over their take from an hour ago. They had about three thousand X pills, twenty-six thousand in cash, and a break down assault rifle with two extra magazines.

It definitely wasn't what Ace expected. His estimate had been a lot higher than the bulk of shit before him. Though at the same time, at least it was a little something to replace a portion of the lost he'd taken thanks to D-nice.

Ace sat in the Cobb County spot he'd purchased specifically for when times were exactly like they were – all around the board difficult and unpredictable.

This was his *fall off the earth* resort, a sanctuary he could retreat to at any given moment. He had kept the house a secret for years, cherishing it as his haven of freedom – a place where he could find solace when his thoughts became too burdensome. Usually, he needed space to himself to work through his troubles. However, given the recent hazardous events, it would now serve as his team's operational base.

6:19 a.m. was the time displayed on the screen of his phone. He quickly scanned through his call log and saw what seemed to be an ongoing list of missed calls from Sassy. The last time he'd spoken to her had been yesterday evening, so he already knew this was bound to happen.

Her worried ass. He laughed on the inside, knowing he'd have to call her the first moment he thought she'd be up – well, before anxiety got the best of her. She'd probably already reached the point of exploding on him. So, it would be expected whenever he finally did call.

Continuing to scroll down the lists of Sassy's calls, he finally paused on a different missed call. Ace now remembered missing it on purpose a few hours ago. She must have been *too* ready for a nigga. He smiled, unable to perceive any other explanation for her hitting him that late, especially if she *so called* had a man as she'd blatantly put it. Surely he was going to find out by calling her at an awkward time as well.

Standing from the chair, Ace glanced over the spoils of war one more time then headed for the bathroom while, at the same time, pressing his thumb down on the call icon. Listening to the ringing, he released all that had waited for hours into the toilet.

"Damn…" he groaned as she answered.

"Hello?" She sounded like he'd just woken her, but her voice was still sexy though.

His manhood jerked upward a little bit at the pleasant sound. "Shouldn't you be getting ready for school?" he asked, flushing the toilet.

"Who is this?"

"Your newfound associate..." He chuckled, realizing she hadn't even bothered to look at the incoming call before answering.

"Ace?" she finally uttered lowly after a brief pause.

"Damn, that was dry. Maybe I need to get at you later?"

"No, no, it's alright. Just early. What time is it?"

"Six thirty," he returned, loving how her voice sounded. He could only imagine the way it would sound when she moaned or orgasmed. His dick instantly went stiff at the thought.

"*Real* early," she said, releasing a little, sexy ass giggle.

"Wow, early to a college girl?"

"I don't go to class until eleven. So yes, early to a college girl. And by the way, why are you up so early?

"Shid, I get up early every morning… most of the time earlier than this."

"Really? Well, what's the reason for calling *me* this early since we both know that this isn't a part of your *early* morning routine?" The way she made it sound seemed as if she was looking for her own little morning spot in his life.

He smiled broadly. "Just returning a missed call from you – which was even *earlier* than this."

"From me?" she questioned as though she'd forgotten about it.

"Nah… from you, girl," he retorted smartly.

There was a moment of silence then, "Oh. Oh, yeah." He guessed she now remembered. "Okay, we can't talk over the phone about it... So, let's say you treat me to breakfast?"

Damn, it wasn't a booty call. He smiled as his manhood went limp. "I see you *used* to getting treated. So, how bout we break that habit with you being the treator?" She most definitely could have gotten breakfast and lunch if she'd had on her mind what he did. But that was her loss.

"Ummm, okay. Well, where would you like to be treated to, Mr. Ace?" She sounded a little reluctant.

"Whatever suits the occasion, Ms. Stacey."

"I like that. Let me get myself together and I'll text you the place in about an hour."

"So, you already have some'n in mind?"

"Something… yes."

"Well, just so you know, I don't eat *anything*."

Stacey chuckled. "Anything would be the last thing."

He liked the counter remark. "Aight, say no more."

Those were the words he ended the call with while he leaned against the sink. Ace tapped the iPhone against his chin, wondering what could possibly be so important that they had to meet in person – *just to talk about it*, as she put it.

It had begun to seem as if something strange was at play. What woman called at two in the morning to discuss business? Which was exactly what their first conversation had been about. They had met face-to-face only once after their initial encounter at the loft. The conversation had centered on her and her associates, though it hadn't been particularly informative; she had spent an hour saying very little. He took this as her way of asserting importance, which he found some-what endearing.

It was odd though. Ever since they'd first spoken a word to each other, she would give off that sexually alluring vibe, sending his mind one way. Then, she'd quickly, and quite easily, switch into straight business mode. Maybe it was her alter ego – or maybe *her game* might have been to arouse you enough to cut your fucking head off when a nigga was too caught in lusting on her sexy ass.

That didn't fit her persona too much though. Of course she was a female with brains yet. in his opinion, just not one with enough brains to maneuver as she was. Evidently, the *people* she often spoke of were for real and obviously pulling the strings like a marionette. For what purpose though?

It was amusing to him. He hadn't agreed to anything, nor mentioned that he would. So, what could possibly be of such urgency to cause her to hit him at two a.m., only to turn around and want to discuss something so... serious that it couldn't be *conversed* about over the phone?

In due time, I'll know, he said to himself, tired of beating his mind up with the perplexing situation.

"Man, I got to pop a few of these," Ace heard Kero say as he stepped back into the living room.

"Cause you a fucking jay." Ace laughed, glancing at the three of them.

Kero looked as if he was more than ready to down a few of them, just to start off with. "Fucking right for the E, nigga. Oh, and the E is for exotic," he finished, causing a few chuckles.

"Shid, I guess all of us finna be some jays then," said Dre, fully aware that all of them popped except Whiteboy.

"Nah, we gone finish this business shit first then maybe think about partying later," Ace spoke with a serious tone. The last thing on his mind right now was getting geeked. He'd been grazed by a bullet, so shit was definitely far from over. He had to be on his toes at all times.

Whiteboy understood exactly what he was thinking. "So, what's the next move?"

The lick they'd just hit, in Ace's eyes, had been nothing more than a mere pinch to the damage he planned on inflicting to his former boss' operations. He wasn't going to settle for anything less than complete annihilation.

Ace figured the next move would be a lot harder once Black found out what happened. That didn't matter in the least to him though. What had to be done – nonetheless – would be done. Point-blank-period.

"We got the drop on his Stone Mountain spot, which should be a nice lil check. But he do got a few more niggas standing guard over the king's treasure, so y'all already know we gone have to be swift and quick. These muthafuckas ain't gone bullshit like homie them..."

Before he could finish, Whiteboy cut in. "Like that matters. The more the merrier."

. . .

SITTING IN HIS RIVERDALE SPOT, BLACK WAS COMFORTABLY BLOWING on some of the city's best Kush as he held the phone up to his ear. He was listening to the most annoying shit he'd heard all week.

This fucking slime ball ass nigga, he thought, continuing to inhale the acrid smoke, hoping it would ease the fury which was growing with every word he heard. He knew this nigga was capable of some messed up shit. Black felt dumb for refusing to accept it as it was. There had been too many signs of treachery and disloyalty.

However, the sole and only reason Black had put up with so much of this guy's bullshit was because of the treacherous deed he'd done before dude could even understand what loyalty was. This had been the main reason he'd taken him under his wing. He felt he owed him and his deceased father at least that, especially after being more than aware that all the responsibility for their permanent separation laid on his very own lap.

"Furg, what's the business, big homie?" Black greeted, giving *some dap to his supplier, who'd just let him into his home.*

"Shit, young boy. What you got going on?" returned Furg, locking *the door back.*

"Shhh, I can't call it. A nigga just trying to get right." Black *smiled shyly as he took a glance around the place, noticing that every-thing occupied the same places as he remembered from a previous visit.*

"If you stop playing and get on this side of the fence, you'd get real right, youngster."

Black smirked. "Man, come on, Furg. You know I like my own."

"How you like your own when your own is nothing?"

With that, Black went silent a moment, understanding the fact that he wasn't trying to be funny or disrespectful. It wasn't Furg's style. He was from the old school and always remained straight forward when making a point. And he'd made one. What Black racked in were mere peanuts compared to the money Furg grossed, which was his sole purpose for being here tonight.

"Anyway..." began Black, blowing the remark off. "What we looking like? You fucking wit me?"

Furg partially chuckled, taking a seat at his dining room table. "You wanted nine, right?"

"That too..." Black's demeanor quickly shifted to a more aggressive stance as he snatched the Glock 9 from his waistline, placing it softly on the table. Then, he took a seat across from his former mentor.

Furg squinted at the pistol unbelievingly. Hard as it was, he nonetheless still managed to keep his smile in place. "Damn, youngsta. I expected this part of the game, but..." He shook his head, though it was not because of the current situation but because he'd wholeheartedly allowed it. "But not from you."

Black smirked perfidiously. "Really? How not, seeing as how you have all this something and I have – in your words – nothing."

He watched Furg carefully, knowing he was calculating his next move, which would be his best, rationalized one. True, Furg was fearless. But as well, he was smart, and the fact that they were in his home, where his only son slept a few feet away, would cause him to be even smarter in his actions.

They sat a moment in silence, both anticipating the next move of the other. Their lives depended on it.

Then, Black decided to break it. "Look, let me make this easy, Furg. Give me all that's in here and that a be that. We'll split ways." He picked the pistol up. "But if you don't want to, then I will kill you and walk down that hallway," he pointed in its direction with the gun, "and kill your beloved little boy. Then, I'ma tear this muthafucka up until I get what I came for. Feel me?" With that, he placed the pistol's marker on his forehead.

Furg didn't move, only stared – the stare of a helpless and hopeless person. He'd been in this game too long to misunderstand the way it would play out once Black laid his hands on that which he demanded.

Hell, once upon a time ago, he'd played the exact same role as Black was. Though not to the hand that fed him. But it was, nonetheless, to a father. He clearly understood it at this point. The best option he had was to barter for his son's life to be spared. Yes, he would sacrifice his very own life to make sure his child made it past four years old.

"Black, I'ma give you what you want — just be a man of honor and give me your word that you will spare the life of my son..."

Furg's proposition stunned him a little, yet it was something he could respect. Of course he would do that for the man who had contributed in so many ways to the establishment of his empire.

Now remembering Furg's words, Black wished he'd have stuck with his first mind, the original plan he'd started out with instead of being merciful to the life he would end up killing years later.

"Well, at least it a be a reunion to look forward to, Furg," Black spoke toward the ceiling, letting the smoke swirl into thin air. Without averting his gaze, he scrolled through the contacts of his phone then ran his finger over the call icon.

After two rings, the voice on the other end answered. "Yo..."

"Say, go pick up the canary and meet me at hollow's ground."

CHAPTER SEVEN

"So, where exactly is this spot ol girl got you all hyped up about?" asked Whiteboy as they traveled on the expressway.

"Out in Jonesborough – right off of Tara Boulevard," Ace replied, thinking about meeting with Stacey. He was in awe by all she'd said, really trying to figure out why Ms. Stacey intended on surprising him with more and more of her awkward actions and revelations.

Actually, he knew it wasn't her but *her people* as she continuously referred to them, each time he implied what *she* wanted. And each time, he couldn't help but wonder why in the hell would a college student be running errands related to something so dangerous, which was precisely what their meeting had covered.

Nah, the real question was what kind of person would send a schoolgirl to discuss hitting up some nigga's spot and killing whoever if need be? The latter was a last resort – as she repeatedly emphasized – but a first if he felt threatened.

None of it made sense. Here, her people were playing the connect role while using her as a middleman – or middlegirl. *For what though?* He couldn't quite say, and had she not mentioned what the goal of the hit would be, he wouldn't have continued to entertain the crazy shit. But over fifty bricks?

That was all he heard. The rest of her words had become inaudible to his ears. Of course he thought about whether or not it was real. Yet, he couldn't conjure no logical reason as to why her, or her people, would waste time lying about something to that extent.

He couldn't see it, so now, they had his undivided attention. Well, at least for the time being. Plenty of his questions would be answered soon enough.

"And what we getting out of this? I mean, our cut?" Whiteboy asked curiously, furrowing his eyebrows at Ace.

That is a good question, Ace was now thinking, realizing he had no idea of how the split would go. He'd asked Stacey the same question, whereas she simply stated, "They'd sort all of that out once it is in their hands."

He smiled, understanding that if a solid agreement hadn't been reached, first and foremost, then some bad business was definitely bound to be the result. And he didn't plan on being the one left with the shit end of the stick, especially if that was what she had in mind.

"Shid, we gonna see when we touch down," Ace finally said, punching the accelerator.

AN HOUR LATER.

Ace and Whiteboy ended up at the top of a dead-end street, which the GPS indicated was their target destination.

The street was deserted besides that of a few quiet homes which lined both sides of the narrow street. The only real difference, as far as he could tell, was that the ones lined on the left side were leveled higher than the ones on the right.

Gazing down at the GPS then back at the row of houses to his right, Ace quickly spotted the one he'd drove an hour and a half to see.

Perfect, he said to himself, pulling the rental slowly away from the stop sign. He paid close attention to the entire scenery, catching sight of a vacant house, which sat three houses down with an adjacent car porch. What made it attractive was that it sat higher than a few of the other houses and a little farther back than them.

"That's the one..." Ace nodded toward it for Whiteboy to see.

As he drove down the quiet, dead-end street passing his target, he noticed two cars were parked in the driveway and what seemed to be a work van under the car porch. The presence of vehicles indicated occupancy, although it offered no insight into how many people resided within it. Nonetheless, it hinted at the fact that there was room for potential activity within the house.

He sped up a little, looking for an opportunity to make a U-turn. Unnoticeably, he slowed the vehicle in front of the parking spot he had in mind then reversed it up the steep driveway until he was under its car porch. But only enough where he'd be able to have a clear sight of the main attraction without being made.

"Bra, you must of been out here before?" Whiteboy questioned, seeing the good position Ace whipped them into.

"Nigga, no. I just pay good attention to my surroundings," Ace said arrogantly, offering him a slick smirk.

"Man, whatever."

Ace heard the clicking of Whiteboy's seat as he adjusted it.

"Shawty, we ain't finna be out here that long. I just want to see the type of muthafuckas we gone have to deal with."

Ace picked up the small binoculars he'd placed in the armrest then set his eyes on the residence.

"Man please, fucking wit you, we'll be on some real stakeout shit. So, while you watch, I'ma sleep. Capeesh?" Whiteboy finished comically.

He couldn't help but to let out a small laugh, while examining the house closely.

Almost two hours had gone by before Ace saw any movement. The front door had opened but without a single body stepping through the threshold. It was something he might have missed if the text message hadn't come through from Sassy. *I love you :).*

He was grateful. She always found a way to keep him focused. Locking back in, he waited to see a body. Ace wondered why the door just hung open with nothing else to be seen. It had been a little more than four minutes now.

"The fuck they doing?" he mumbled under his breath, becoming partially irritated. He was ready to see who would become the next victims on his list. Lord knew he needed more hits.

A light-skinned dude appeared from within, rubbing his eyes as he proceeded down a few stairs. Then, a second dude came out, swiveling backwards like he was speaking his last peace to whoever remained on the inside.

"The fuck!" Ace had spoken loud enough to cause Whiteboy to stir from his little nap.

"What's up?" he asked, yawning and massaging the bridge of his nose.

"Hol up. I'm tryna see now..." Ace replied, watching the men as they passed words back-and-forth. At first, he didn't believe the second dude who stepped out was who he thought it was. But his suspicion had been confirmed once he turned all the way around, followed out by another person.

His smile became broader instantaneously. The realization of what he was seeing began to set in.

Pee Pee and D. Ace stared at the two incredulously for a minute, letting his mental attempt to piece together the puzzle before his very eyes, and that wouldn't take long. These two were never at a spot unless the *say so* came from the mouth of Black, which meant that this particular abode was, nonetheless, Black's – one Mal had failed to mention. However, a piece remained missing. Why would Stacey's people put him on this place? And how did they even know about it?

Flipping it all in his mind, Ace mused over the possibility that it could have been a setup. Black had hundreds of connections with various people, far and wide, but the smell of it wasn't matching a conniving scheme to fuck him over. Nah, if Black was using these muthafuckas to get at him, he could have easily executed that because numerous opportunities had previously been presented. All of which was due to Ace letting his guard down the majority of the time, like when he thought he was on safe grounds at the loft.

That isn't it, so what is? he asked himself. His mind jumped into gear, quickly plotting on a devise which would leave both parties emptyhanded while he laughed all the way to the bank. This was a major plus in his book.

"Ain't nothing better than crossing a crosser." He chuckled, watching Pee Pee and the other guy drive away while D stepped back into the very house they would be in soon.

CHAPTER EIGHT

ollow's ground wasn't the exact name of the place located in Kennesaw, Georgia. Yet it had been designated as such due to the cavernous spaces beneath the surface. Some were filled with corpses Black had ordered hits on, and some were patiently waiting to be filled.

The scenery was like one of those spooky ones you'd see in scary movies with one little house surrounded by the big, gloomy trees protruding from the soft, moist dirt.

The fog never seemed to leave, which only added more mystique to the area, making it hard at times to maneuver down the dirt road that led directly to the house.

Black had ran across the murky place in an advertisement ad for *cheap, unwanted property*. After paying it a visit, he knew it would be prefect for exactly what he planned on using it for.

He sat in a wooden chair, spinning a bottle on the table, patiently waiting for the arrival of the three visitors who were to show very shortly now. He couldn't wait to take care of *his* loose knot. This, he felt, was a little more than needed. It had been a while since he'd actually gotten his own hands dirty.

In a sense, this particular situation almost resembled that of the one with Furg – considering someone close until their selfishness broke the ties of loyalty, trust, and sometimes love. But street niggas knew there were only two places to direct the latter toward – your kids and your money. Anywhere else would be your very own fuck-up. This was something he learned from – like the situation with Ace.

Black laughed to himself, thinking about Ace, quickly remembering how Ace had beaten Reno damn near to death with the crowbar – the same one he glanced over, which held its ground propped up against the wall. He'd kept it after all these years because, to him, it had become a thing which symbolized the way niggas were to be dealt with for their disloyal actions – exactly what it had been used for then and exactly what it was about to be utilized for tonight.

It even, after all this time, still had the blood of Reno on it. Black figured washing it would destroy the significance of it. To him, every perfidious muthafucka would be remembered by the trace of their own blood on the object. Which was to be drawn by fierce blows delivered from the iron instrument.

"You a sick ass nigga," he spoke to himself, adding a small chuckle before finally bringing the bottle to a halt. Checking the time, Black touched an icon on the touch screen, making a call. Then, he heard car tires treading over the gravel out front. *Good.* He made his way to the front door to welcome his guest. He was already aware he'd have to give them enough room to enter. Two would be walking, the third dragged in by the ankles.

Upon opening, he watched the dark Navigator come to a stop inches away from the porch. Two guys immediately hopped out, moving straight for the rear in cadence. Lifting the back, they both reached in, snatching the third individual out.

Black smiled with amusement, watching them drag him up the stairs. He stepped to the side as they brought him into the place and released the garbage in the center of the living room floor. He slammed the door after the two left and walked over to the main reason for the occasion. *Look at you.* He stared down disgustedly at the guy who squirmed like a fish did when at the point of dying on land. Then, he snatched the cloth from his head.

Reno gazed upward, rapidly blinking his eyelids as if he hadn't seen light in days. A dull sound exuded from him, but there was nothing more due to the duct tape covering his mouth.

Black grimaced. Blood and sweat streaked and mixed down his face and neck, but that wasn't what caused the expression to overcome Black's face. It was the cowardly, pleading look he gave the man who stood above.

"They say the eyes will never lie," Black told him, staring him directly into his eyes. "Now, why would you, out of all people, be so afraid to see me, I wonder?"

Reno's body began to tremble as his eyes stayed on the last person he wanted to see.

Black walked into the kitchen, picking up a knife, and went back to his prey. He noticed the closer he got, the wider Reno's eyes got, seeming as if they had no limit.

"Are we going to play nice – or naughty?" He laughed, removing the tape from his mouth.

Reno became stiff, making no attempt to respond. His mind was too busy trying to figure out why he'd been handed to the Grim Reaper. He trailed over some of the last few movements he'd made and hadn't seen one that would place him in this current predicament – though he did, and was continuing to, help the agents build a case against Black.

Reno was certain he hadn't been found out about – or had he? He was always careful, extra cautious, of their dealings to the point that if someone knew, it would have come from *them* or him. He was positive that neither had happened.

Finishing, Black shook the tape from his hand.

"Black, ma…"

"Shhh…" Black quickly cut him short. "Let me start…" He paused briefly to grab the chair he'd previously sat in. Black placed it right in front of Reno. "You know I fucked with you, right? But it seems to be a one-way thing."

"Black, bra, you kn…"

"My nigga, let me finish. Now, don't say you fuck wit me or that you got a lot of love for me cause on some real shit, if you did, you wouldn't be doing the shit you do – or did – however you want to look at it. Seeing the predicament you're in, honestly can you say it was worth it, Reno?" Black leaned back in the chair, signaling for Reno to defend himself, even though it would be in vain.

Reno was confused, having not the slightest clue as to how to respond. *What is Black talking about?* he wondered and knew Black all too well to think he was just making up some bullshit. One thing every person understood when it came down to Black was that he wasn't the type to beat around the bush, especially when one of his *own's* life lingered within the interim of life or death. Wherever he went with his words, he always had a reason to.

This *reason* still remained unclear to Reno as his words held no motivation to leave his throat. At this point, they wouldn't matter. He was already aware he wasn't brought out here just to utter things that could possibly save his life. His fate had been decided, and right now, he only wished it would be quick and painless.

"Man, Black... Man, you got it. I don't know what happened or what I did, but my nigga, I still got love..." Before he could finish, Black stomped him in the face without leaving the chair. Reno let out a muffled sound as his head snapped backwards into the wooden floor.

"Nigga!" Black shouted, instantly becoming furious. "Fuck all that, nigga. What? You think I don't know what the hell you been doing? Like I don't know who you been popping to, muthafucka. I'm Black!" He went silent. Trying to regain his composure, he calmly got up and walked over to fetch the iron fist of disloyalty.

Taking his seat again, he placed the crowbar between his legs as if it was a walking cane.

The steel had Reno's full attention. The red crimson flowed from both nostrils freely. He began to speak. "Bla-Black, I swear I don't know what you talking bout, bra. I..." he uttered, dumbfounded. Though now, he was at the conclusion that Black possessed full knowledge of his secrets. However, he refused to man up and say that he was a snitch and at that, say that he was ratting out the only person who'd ever done anything for him. He couldn't find it in his heart to actually tell him to his face. Fuck what the outcome would be.

And the funny part about it was he was definitely ignorant of the person who was patiently waiting on the cue to show his face.

Black smiled down at him, realizing that he'd really grounded himself on that belief. "Okay, that's your story. That's the move. Do you remember when Fury died?" questioned Black, allowing him enough time to visit memory lane before all of it ceased to exist.

Reno laid there and shook his head. He couldn't understand what that had to do with any of this.

"Where was you?"

"Wha-what you mean?" Reno asked, confoundedly. The question was more than odd.

"Nigga, where the fuck was you at?"

Reno remained silent, trying to figure out where he was going with this shit. Surely Black was trying to fuck with his mind. "I-I was four, man. How…"

"Nigga, do you know or not?" Black growled, irritated.

"They say I-I was in the bed asleep."

Black grinned. "Really? So, you was napping while some nigga just killed your ol man?"

"Black, I was four," Reno uttered, not wanting to die but ready for whatever to happen.

"Oh, just four?" Black chuckled. "Aight, do you know where I was?"

Reno gave him the strangest look, which quickly became replaced with fear and curiosity. Why would that matter? He had a gut feeling he somehow knew. It had been a secret all these years, the answer to a question that roamed the highways of his mind. "Nah..." he finally uttered, spitting a clot of blood inches away from Black's Timberland boot.

Black's smile grew bigger once Reno asked him, "You tell me?" He admired the new look in his eyes now. It was a look which spoke of hate, betrayal, and anger – a look he'd never seen Reno express, except for one time.

"You know, you gave me that same exact glare at Furg's funeral. It was like you knew. Like you woke up that night and witnessed it first-hand..." Tears began to fill Reno's eyes as Black continued to fill him in on the details of the past. "Anyway, I was there. I burned 'em," he told him flatly with a devilish smirk. "I killed Furg and took all he had – every single thing." He paused as he aimed the crowbar at Reno's face.

"Even you. Not because I wanted to. Shid, I was gone do both of y'all, but Furg pleaded – sacrificed his own life, like the good nigga he was, for the life of his only son to be spared. How could I not respect that? How could I not fuck wit him when he was the one who'd put me where I am? That was the sole reason I took your disloyal ass in," he finished aggressively.

"Disloyal?" Reno retorted. "Nigga, you killed my pops and kept me at your side as your do boy. Nigga, I should of been did some fucked-up shit to you a long time ago..."

Black was astounded by the remark. "Yeah, and I should of went with my first mind. But be grateful, bitch ass nigga. At least I didn't manipulate you into killing your father like I did with Ace."

"Fuck you!" Reno clamored, tears running down the side of his face. "Nigga, I wasn't nothing but loyal to you an-and that's how you do?"

"Nah, that's how you do..." Black turned in his chair and aimed the crowbar at the first bedroom door, which was beginning to open.

Reno stared at the figure who was appearing from the darkness. At first, it was only a big blur moving forward. The closer it got, the clearer it became. *Oh, shit*, he thought, watching the dude slowly make his way across the floorboard. He now became aware of why Black had made his accusations. How these two were connected, he couldn't fathom.

Black laughed at the expression on Reno's face as Agent Swift stopped next to him. "Ion think I need to introduce you two, do I?" Black asked.

Reno's entire body became rigid. His mouth suddenly went dry. Just when he thought Black would get his, in the end, all hopes of revenge flew out the window. It was for certain with this guest appearance.

"How are you doing, Mr. Baits?" Swift asked, smiling down at Reno, who couldn't do anything but stare in disbelief.

"Please don't be shy now." Black could tell he had cotton in his mouth. He wanted nothing more than to see how he would respond to this shocking revelation.

Reno said nothing, like he was a fucking mute.

"Well, in case you're wondering how this came about," Swift said, gesturing with his arm, "here's the secret. I work for Black – or rather been working for him for quite a while now." He chuckled as he squatted down in front of Reno. "Now, this is how you fit in. The reason for him passing you over to me is because… Well, I needed to clear up a couple of dirt tracks that were trying to become permanent trails…. I needed something, you know, to make *us* look good for a few top heads, and I'll give it to you. You did a hell of a job. Well, to be more frank about it, it was *too* good of a job, which is why you're in this unfortunate position now. But good luck in the next life," he finished, leaving Reno with the feeling of being all the way around the board *played*.

"And now," Black began, finally standing from the chair, "you're a useless ass nigga to both of us..." He spit, causing the saliva to land directly on the side of his face.

"Man, fuck you, Black. You set me up to do this," Reno snapped, more so pleading, after grasping the fact that Black had been the one pulling the strings through the whole ordeal, and he'd played it as if this outcome was decided from the start.

"No, nigga. I gave you the opportunity to play yourself, and you did. Reno, this shit was all on you."

Those were his last words. He lifted the crowbar and relentlessly began to bash the side of his head in with multiple strikes of brute force that quickly caused his skull to give way and crush under the pressure.

CHAPTER NINE

"Late ass nigga," D mouthed after reading the text message. The morning breeze brushed against him as he removed the cigarette from behind his ear and proceeded in firing it up.

At only nine fifteen in the morning, he already felt that his day had started out good. And he'd set his mind on making sure that the rest of his day was even better. Though he knew it would be because he had a special date with a stripper named *Exotica*.

"Um–mmm–mmhh!" He shook his head, thinking about the foreign, fat ass she possessed as he released nicotine smoke into the air.

Then, he heard a female's voice say, "Damn!"

The sound was sexy to him, causing him to snap his head toward the direction he thought it came from. At first, he couldn't see her, only the tail end of a burgundy Lexus. Moving into another position, he saw the entire vehicle with its hood up. It was a few houses down, parked at the side of the street.

He pulled on the cigarette again, stepping off of the porch, wanting to get a glimpse of exactly who the voice belonged to. And there she was, doing something no female he could think of, knew how to do.

Suspiciously, D scrutinized the area, searching for anything out of place. After being satisfied, he began to make his way over the grass and down toward the short, thick, caramel complexion chick in front of the Lexus.

Good God! He huffed to himself, taking the Newport from his lips. D found it hard to avert his gaze. She leaned in under the hood, leaving her perfectly round apple bottom visible for the entire world to admire.

"Damn!" he exclaimed in a whisper, glancing backwards at the spot. He was more than aware that his body wasn't supposed to leave the confines of the house unless another person was there. His luck. He'd been the only one present for the past few hours.

But damn, she only a few feet away, he began to think, taking another brief glance around the quiet cul-de-sac. Nothing.

He wanted to go against offering any assistance to the fine ass female, but his manhood wouldn't let him. It throbbed at the possible future of satisfaction.

Fuck it, ain't nobody out here to even think of trying no shit. He had to reassure himself as he proceeded in her direction.

Damn, Ace gone replace this shit. Ariel noticed the smear of grease on the skirt which accompanied her frame nicely as she leaned under the hood. This was the first part of Ace's plan, but she didn't expect to get dirty while doing it.

Ariel had been out here for every bit of an hour, waiting on her target to approach and indulge her in a slight conversation, which would definitely be to his own downfall. Once she caught a glimpse of him stepping out of the residence, she knew this was her cue to put on a good show – something she did anyway.

Peeking around the hood, Ariel could tell that she'd gotten his undivided attention with her brief *Damn!* Now, all she needed was for him to fetch after the unknown, like dogs were used to doing.

She eyed him closely as he made his way across the yard. Ariel inched the skirt up her thighs some, revealing a beautiful part of her ass that could make any dick stiffen.

"And you going to be the grand finale, Mama," she uttered, gazing down at her fat camel toe.

Ariel moved around to the side of the vehicle, pretending as if she hadn't noticed the big man. Leaning over even farther, she slightly bounced her booty upwards, applying a little seductive wiggle.

Between the small gap of the hood, at the bottom of the windshield, she could see him. "Smuch, smuch, come here, boy," she whispered, playfully calling him as if he were an actual dog. Well, all men were if you asked her.

Within no time, he doggishly responded to her body movements. Ariel watched as he continued in her direction. She smiled, realizing how easy and eager he was to aid in his very own demise. Now, all she needed was to keep him occupied long enough for Ace and the boys to do their part. Which was to enter and secure the vulnerable spot before he returned. And the look on his face made it apparent that keeping his attention would be a piece of cake.

"Damn, bae..." she heard him say as he made it close to her. Playing her part perfectly, Ariel waited another second before acknowledging the remark.

"Excuse you?" she responded as if his comment had been vulgar. Usually, she would return a disrespectful line, but there was a mission to accomplish.

Ridiculous, she thought after watching his retinas fall exactly where she wanted them to, just not as fast as they had.

Stupid dog, she wanted to say yet knew better. Pulling her skirt lower to cover the magnificent print, she repeated, "Excuse you?"

"Oh, my bad. I meant no harm, beautiful," he told her after the covering up brought his horny ass back to reality. "How you though?"

"Good... and you are?" She folded her arms across her chest a little snobbishly. It was all part of the image she had to paint.

He smiled, thinking he'd fell into the presence of one of the finest women in the city. "They call me D..."

"And you want?" She cocked her head to the side, irritated. Ariel knew that to keep any dude's attention, all a girl had to do was act sexily stuck up.

"Damn, baby girl, it's like that?"

"Of course to strangers."

"Well, strangers mostly be in *strange* places, and this seems to be," he glanced around at the surrounding area, "a very nice neighborhood."

Reluctantly, she gave a small smile, quite amused that the big chunk of stupidness possessed a little charm. "*Well,* bad things happen in very nice places too."

"True, but you got my word, Ma…" He placed his hand over his heart, like he was intending on taking an oath. "I'm not one of them *bad things* that could happen."

Ariel laughed a little, not because he seemed to be doing his best to put her at ease but because he had no idea that he was only playing himself. "Okay then, Mr. Nice, you walked all the way over here to do what exactly?"

"*To,*" he mocked with a smirk, "help you, seeing as how a beautiful lady as yourself shouldn't be under no hood doing a man's job." He then pumped his chest up, full of himself.

"Well, thanks, but no help is needed to check something as small as my oil."

He appeared to be a little disappointed in a playful way. "Okay then, Miss?"

"Venom…"

"Oh, so you poisonous?"

"To both the bad and the nice," she said seductively with a little something else riding her voice.

"For real?" He furrowed his eyebrows curiously.

She chuckled. "Venom is my stage name."

"Stage name?" He loved the way that sounded because strippers were right up his alley.

"Yes. I dance."

Yes! His mental shouted. "Really? Where at?"

"Pink Pony South, nosy," she told him with a smirk.

"I'm just asking, damn." With that, he lifted his hands placatingly.

Ariel twisted her lips. "Well, since you over there wanting to conversate, how bout you be useful and check my oil – which you asked to do by the way."

D laughed. "You fye now."

"How? Because I took your advice?"

"Nah, but a few seconds ago, you didn't need my help on something so small, remember?" he cajoled.

"I mean, what's the point in all this talk and no work?" She stepped back, giving him more than enough room. Last thing she wanted was for his little man to get happy and bust from a simple brush.

"My type of girl." He smiled then took a dip under the hood. "By the way, you should know that I usually don't get my hands dirty with shit like this…"

The rest was blah, blah, blah. Her attention was on Ace and Whiteboy creeping across the street, right through the yard. Then, late as usual, Spain ran in their direction two seconds before the big man lifted his fat head back up.

"You were saying what?" she asked, easing close enough to almost rub her breasts up against him.

"Ummm…" He bit down on his bottom lip like he couldn't wait to eat her alive. "Your oil looks straight."

"I bet it is…" she mouthed sexily, gripping a handful of his manhood – well, a majority of the denim material he wore.

He released a light gasp, ready to acknowledge what the gesture insinuated. Instantly, he became exhilarated. "Damn, bae…" He attempted to pull her even closer to him, but she quickly pivoted around, slamming the hood down.

"Thank you!" Ariel winked, offering a smile as she moved past him.

"Shhh, shawty, what's up?" he questioned, a bit confused, wondering where the mood had gone so fast.

A small chuckle escaped her lips before she responded, "Nothing." She shut the car door.

D stood there a moment, lost. He eyed his escaping satisfaction as she pulled away, obviously laughing at his facial expression.

Ariel wanted to give him another tease for the hell of it. *Damn*, her smile broadened after realizing that he'd never get another shot at some pussy.

Stupid bitch! D now realized what was taking place after watching the supposed *Venom* maneuver her car around and up the street.

"Fuck!" he growled, using every muscle in his legs. *Dumb ass nigga,* he began to curse himself. All along, this hoe had been a decoy for whatever slick shit she had going on. Surely if that was the case, the bitch would pay and whoever else was involved.

Finally making it to the first step out of breath, D reached down at his waist for his strap.

Shit! There was no fucking way he'd left the Millennium nine on the coffee table *inside* the house. He'd just remembered.

Hesitant a moment, he glanced around at the construction tools and poles which were scattered about the porch. If someone lurked within, his chance of successfully grabbing the pistol was slim to none. But he would have to take his chances, he knew, grabbing an iron rod from the pile.

Of course, he more than understood that he couldn't be still alive and something had gone wrong with Black's shit. Death at the hands of Black would certainly be much worse than anything another mutha-fucka had to offer.

This shit 'pose to be under construction. Ace stepped beyond the threshold, instantly noticing the big ass flat screen and an entire – expensive looking – home theater system.

Pointing, he signaled for Spain to check the rear of the house while him and Whiteboy found positions up front. Ace wanted to duck off somewhere close, near the entrance, so they'd be able to take D swiftly, leaving no room for him to buck.

This shit is too easy. Ace wanted to smile, imagining the face D would have once he realized who'd been waiting on him.

Whiteboy moved to the right, disappearing into the living room closet. The wait was on.

A few seconds later, Ace could hear footsteps shuffle on the front porch. He attempted to make out exactly where he was but was unable to.

He trying to be smart. Ace smiled. No matter what D did, or how strategic he tried to be, it wouldn't prevent the inevitable.

The latch on the door clicked. Ace could hear the floor squeak under the weight of the big guy's feet. All of which amounted to his cue.

Speedily, Ace sprang into action from behind the wall, quickly aiming his pistol at the target. "Nigga, drop that shit!" Ace barked menacingly, looking at the pole, then boring into D's shocked eyes.

"Ace..." D iterated awkwardly, exhibiting an appalling look, clearly ignoring the statement. "M-man, what's up, Ace?" he stuttered, clutching the rod even tighter. He'd known Ace since Black first took him in, so he was more than aware of the circumstances.

"Ain't shit up, nigga. You know what the fuck is shaking. Either drop that shit or I'ma burn your ass."

D figured he'd probably do that anyway. This was Ace, who cared less about how defenseless a person was. He'd do them on the strength. Then, the fact that the little war him and the boss had going on was far from being settled. At this moment, there wasn't a doubt in D's mind that he'd become a martyr today.

Fuck!!! How could he be so gullible, thinking with his dick head? Out of all the dumb shit he had done, this was by far the dumbest. His chances of survival were below none. Yet he wouldn't just go easily. He had to try them. With that, he remembered something. His eyes darted to the coffee table, which stood no more than four feet away with the Millennium on it.

"D, don't tell me you've gotten that stupid. For real?" Ace noticed – for the first time – the pistol he and Whiteboy had missed upon entering.

"Ace, man..." were the only words to exit his mouth while the pupils of his eyes switched between Ace and the pistol.

"Okay…" Ace smirked, willing to let him try it. He didn't want to shoot him with the door wide open. Anyone close enough would definitely hear it. But if he tried it, none of that shit would matter. "Go for it then, nigga."

Without hesitating, D slung the pole at Ace, quickly scrambling for the table.

BOOM!!!

The gunshot rang out, and D's body jerked backwards from the impact of the bullet tearing through his shoulder.

Whiteboy came from the closet, he took one big step before delivering D a solid kick to the face.

"Aghh," D squawked, futilely continuing to reach. His life depended on it.

"Fuck ass nigga!" Ace snarled, quickly retrieving the weapon, landing a few ruthless kicks to his midsection. Then, he completed the attack with a firm soccer kick to the face. "Find some'n to tie this nigga up with," he told Whiteboy.

"At least you tried…" Ace chuckled, staring down at D, who gripped his shoulder while blood gushed from his nose and mouth. Ace thought about opening him up a little more, but he needed him conscious.

"Man, fuck, this gonna have to work," Whiteboy said, grabbing an extension cord.

Turning the three-hundred-pound man onto his stomach, Ace put a knee on his neck then placed the muzzle to his head as Whiteboy wrapped the cord tightly around his thick wrists.

"Spain…" Ace called out. Immediately, he heard him close in. "Watch the front. A gone hit if she see somebody heading this way, aight?"

Spain said nothing, only gave a nod of the head.

After watching Whiteboy finish, Ace knew it was time to get down to business. Tucking both guns down into his jeans, he gazed down at the heavy task at hand. "Let's move him to the kitchen." With that, they gripped him under his arms.

"Ace, baby…" His mouth began pleading as they dragged him

around the couch and onto the tile floor. "Ace, man, don't do this — this me."

Ace was amused by the fact that he actually had the nerve to say such. "Nigga, I wonder if you would of felt the same if you would of made it to the pistol."

"Ace… Man, what would you have done if you was in my shoes?"

"My point exactly." Ace went to retrieve the pole then stepped over to the stove.

"Ace! Man please, whatever you want, man, you can have it," D pleaded, hoping he could evade what Ace was apparently intending.

"Chill…" He smiled threateningly. "We gone get to that."

This nigga here crazy. Whiteboy leaned against the counter, staring at Ace, trying to figure out which part of his body the heated metal would brand first.

"Say, White…" Ace twirled the rod to ensure the entire tip rose in temperature. "Hold his head sideways. Oh, and watch ya hand." He chuckled.

Saying nothing, Whiteboy hesitated a moment then cautiously did as instructed.

"Ace! Come on, man. Don't do this, man!" D cried out, face flat against the tile floor.

Ace grinned, ignoring his pleas, continuing to rotate the metal. This was about to be a sight to see.

D's howls echoed louder. He began to kick and wiggle uncontrollably as the rod made its way toward his face.

"Nigga, stop!" Whiteboy growled, landing a stiff punch to the side of the man's neck. But it was to no avail.

"Aghhh!!!" he screamed out. The metal caused his skin to sizzle while it cruised across, stopping only after a streak of pale flesh ran the length of his face.

Ace's eyebrows furrowed, amazed by the swift change in the texture of the wound. He definitely would add this technique to his arsenal of 'ways to torture.'

"Shit…" Whiteboy huffed, turning away from the irritating smell of charred skin.

D whimpered like a real-fucking-baby.

"Now, you can tell me where it's at — or..." The corners of Ace's mouth inched upward. "Or we experiment with this again." He waited a moment then quickly became impatient with the big man's cry of pain. It seemed as if his point hadn't gotten across the first time.

"Aight, say no mo." Ace placed the rod back over the stove.

D's eyes mooned at the sight. "Fuck, o-okay, man. It's-it's in da attic," he stuttered between sobs.

"What, nigga?" Ace pretended like he was about to make another brutal laceration

"Man, it's in the attic! It's in the fucking attic!" he cried out, letting the tears pour freely.

"Bet..." Ace smirked, laying the pole mere inches away from his head. He wanted him to have a constant reminder. "I'ma go look, and if you playing, the next time I'ma put your fucking eye out with it, feel me?"

D barely nodded his cranium once Whiteboy released him. Badly, he wished it was anybody in the word besides Ace playing Hannibal Lecter.

Walking into the hallway, Ace immediately laid eyes on the door to the attic. He bobbed his head up and down, hoping for D's sake that truth had fallen from his lips.

Damn. He noticed that the string to pull it down was more than short and out of his reach. Ace's eyes swept over the interior of the hallway in search of a solution. Nothing.

Quickly, he moved for the rooms. *Nada* in the first one, but the second room had a stepping stool which he figured they'd been using to do the same. Then again, D's big ass was probably big enough to reach and grab it without any assistance.

Placing it where he needed, Ace lifted a foot then heard an agonizing scream. *The fuck?* He sprinted for the kitchen, only to find Whiteboy dragging the pole across D's scalp.

In a state of trepidation, D let out moans of extreme suffering while tears spewed wildly from his eyes. Ace shook his head.

"What? You thought I was gone let you be the only one having fun?" Whiteboy smiled.

"Don't kill 'em. We still might need him, stupid," Ace hissed over his shoulder as he walked off, trying to keep a straight face. "Always got to do something," Ace said to himself, taking the first step onto the stool. Grasping the line, Ace tugged it downward then unfolded the ladder mounted to its door.

Damn, this shit small as fuck, he thought after realizing he wouldn't be able to fully stand. He'd have to crawl over the planks. Ace adjusted the pistols until they felt comfortable then began to maneuver around in search of a light switch.

The entire area was shrouded in pitch blackness, all except for the hole he'd entered, which helped none. Moments later, he located exactly what he was looking for.

"Please, man!" He heard D yelp loudly. Ace chuckled, knowing that Whiteboy would torture him until the shit landed in their hands or he died, whichever came first.

Flicking on the light switch, he noticed that only a portion of the space illuminated, exactly where he was in the center of.

He gazed around, not seeing anything of interest. Peering harder, Ace could see that little square spaces dipped inward on the outskirts of the boards he was on. *And there you are,* he teased, carefully moving over the first squares. The light slowly faded with every few inches he covered. That wouldn't deter him from gaining the greatest gifts any true hustler could possess.

Staring down into the squared compartments, he found it hard to see anything. The rays from the light threw his shadow over them, which only caused more vagueness. Dipping his head lower and squinting his eyes for a better look, Ace could see that layers of installation filled the bottom of the boxes. His intuition led him to lift it. *Nothing!*

Quickly, he began checking the ones surrounding it. They rendered the same results —_nothing. After the ninth one, he became furious. The stuff Whiteboy had done would be considered child's play to what he was intending to unleash on him.

Spinning around quickly, his jaw bones clenched as he crawled back onto the board. D was definitely about to experience torture worse than the shit executed on terrorists at Guantanamo Bay.

"Shhh…" he let out as the board shifted and lifted from the force applied by his knee. Startled a bit, he quickly gripped the closest plank then drew back enough to let the board crash back down.

Slick ass nigga. Immediately, a big smile spread across his face. He used a hand to slide the wood from its original place. The light shined down into the square like this had been a blessing from God himself — the blessing he'd come for.

"Beau-ti-ful," he exclaimed, elated and a little mesmerized at the sight of the neatly laid blocks of cocaine. This was unbelievable. He had to touch it to make sure he wasn't dreaming.

Ace smiled, truly amazed at how his luck had dramatically changed. Climbing back down the ladder, he shook his head slightly. They were back on in a major way and, at the same time, majorly causing a gigantic dent into Black's business plans.

"Talking bout killing two birds with one fucking stone…" Ace laughed, stepping back into the kitchen.

"Spain," Ace pulled the van keys from his pocket, "go get the whip. Back it up the driveway."

Putting his attention on D, Ace was ready to kill another bird.

"D-D-D…" He chuckled with an accompanying clap every time as he pronounced it. "Man, I fucks witcha — I mean, like really though." Ace knelt close to his ear as if he intended on letting him in on a secret. "My nigga, I love ya." He laughed. "I fucking love ya…" Aggressively, he grabbed his cranium, planting a kiss on his bald head before shoving it into the floor.

"What's better?" questioned Whiteboy, curious of the unusual happiness coming from Ace. Evidently, he'd found the jackpot.

Ace looked at Whiteboy, his vibe becoming a little overzealous. "Nigga, we bout to be muthafucking *ri-ich*!"

"Damn, that much?"

"Man, hell yeah!"

"Fucking right, but what we gonna do with this nigga?" Of course

Whiteboy already knew the answer to that. However, he was just a little curious as to the how.

"Shid…" Ace smiled at a thought. "Maybe we can leave him here. That way he can tell *big, bad* Black who did it."

"Man, Ace… Man, my word. I promise, Ace, ain gone say s…"

"Nigga, I want you to tell him." Ace wanted his former boss to know he'd been the reason for his big loss. Though at the same time, he felt it would be better if he left him lost on all accounts.

Surely, he'd be the last person he would think had knowledge of this little spot.

After loading three duffle bags with twenty some bricks apiece —_more than Ace expected — they were about to work on the fourth until Spain's phone blared to life.

"Yeah…" he answered after letting Ace and Whiteboy know who it was.

Ace stared at his young protégé tentatively, wondering who had been spotted cruising the street. Spain quickly stepped over to the blinds and peered out.

"What up?" Ace questioned eagerly.

"Man, some niggas coming our way," Spain said, watching the vehicle pull into the driveway.

"Shit," Ace huffed, snatching both pistols from his waistline. Shit was about to get real. "Who you see?"

"Four niggas in a whip just pulled up."

Before Ace thought of it, Whiteboy moved over to D, stepping down on his neck. "Nigga, who the fuck you expecting?"

D's pain and suffering quickly contorted into a weak laughter.

"Y'all niggas done fucked up. Y'all finna die in this bitch. All for playing around with the wrong muthafucka," he spit out as menacingly as he could.

"You figure?" were the only two words Whiteboy uttered before grabbing the butcher's knife from the counter. Pressing down onto the side of his face, he plunged the blade into his throat, shredding skin and flesh, severing his head farther apart from his body.

"GUESS MOMMY HAVE TO SAVE THE DAY ONCE AGAIN," ARIEL mumbled to herself, thinking about the last time she surprised the opposition.

Parking a few feet from the edge of the driveway, Ariel pulled the M11 from the floor of the car. "Let's put in this work, baby." She kissed the submachine gun then snatched back the slide, launching a round into the chamber.

Ariel eyed the vehicle in front of the van Ace and them had planned on leaving in. She watched as the dudes got out, guns in hand. They were all gazing at the suspicious vehicle which they all probably knew wasn't supposed to be there.

They hadn't approached the van yet, just stood there, mumbling words back-and-forth amongst each other. Their hesitation was her cue to introduce herself.

"Excuse me…" she called out in a real feminine manner, which nonetheless grabbed all of their attention. "Do one of y'all know where…" She pretended to reach for a piece of paper then came out with the M11 and began firing relentlessly.

Hitting the one close to her, she swung the gun between the others, who were scrambling for cover. Consecutive rounds hit the car as if they were trying to dig through to the other side where two were hiding. The guy who ducked low in front of the car began to aimlessly shoot back over the hood.

"Bitch…" she growled, hoping the fifty round clip wouldn't run dry before the gang got out.

"LET'S GET IT!" ACE YELLED THROUGH THE CLOTH WRAPPED AROUND the lower half of his face.

Opening the door, he quickly noticed the three dudes crouched down in front of the car, now taking futile shots at Ariel, who had the full court press down on them niggas.

Aiming, he shot the first of the bunch twice, causing one of them to dive across the front seat of the car. The other guy sprinted like a bat out of hell from the ambush.

Ace continued to shoot as he made his way down the porch stairs, keeping one pistol aimed at the car and the other at the corner of the house. He smirked, realizing that at this very moment he was looking like Antonio Banderas in *Desperado* with Spain on his heels, toting two duffle bags of coke.

"White, hold 'em down," he barked, keeping eyes on the two dudes' positions while backpedaling toward the van.

But Whiteboy was already on it with the AK he'd acquired from one of the back rooms. He swung the muzzle toward the edge of the house, sending a few rounds before snapping his head backwards at the sound of screeching tires. It was Ariel backing up the street. Focusing back on the corner, he continued to shoot at it in hopes that the bullets would go through and through, catching his targets. Yet it was quite obvious that they weren't because the guy's hand continuously appeared from the other side, letting of two rounds at a time.

Ace shot over the van's door at the car's only occupant, who apparently had given up. Then, he heard the van's door slide backwards. Quickly dropping a pistol on the seat, he brought the vehicle to life.

Hearing the motor growl, Whiteboy sent three more rounds toward the edge as he began to step backwards.

"Nigga, come on!" Ace screamed, pushing open the passenger door.

Slapping the gear shift in reverse, Ace pushed down on the accelerator, slamming into a wall. Then, right when he was about to put it in drive, he caught sight of the nigga taking aim at them with a choppa from the back door of the car.

"Fuck!" Ace shouted, ducking toward the middle section with Whiteboy as bullets pierced the windshield and through anything they touched.

Stomping as hard as he could on the gas pedal, Ace rammed the front of the car, forcing the entire vehicle to slide backwards a little.

The firing ceased, and Whiteboy decided to take advantage of this brief opportunity before dude thought there was a chance that he'd become Black's victor of the day. He fired, sending the nigga with the choppa fleeing for the rear. Out of instinct, Whiteboy used the other pistol to halt the other nigga who'd finally come from the side, busting.

Unhesitatingly, Ace rammed the van into the wall a second time then turned the steering wheel hard to the right and stomped the accelerator.

Whiteboy blasted away aimlessly. The van hit the corner of the vehicle, knocking the bumper off as they slid across the lawn. Finally, they made it to the street.

Ace wheeled the van like he was a real getaway driver, desperately trying to put distance between them and dude who was appearing from the side of the car. The choppa's sight was locked on them.

The van would only receive a few more wild rounds before they were off the street and on their way with a — somewhat — successful lick.

Damn, we was lucky, Ace thought after letting his eyes run over Ariel for a moment. He was more than grateful that she'd been there with them today. If she hadn't, there was no telling how the situation would have played out with the unexpected entourage or the shot-up van, something they had to quickly ditch if they didn't want any more unwanted trouble.

She had definitely been their life saver on more than one occasion, but today — to him — she was Jesus. The way she held it down, he could do nothing besides bow in respect to her feminine prowess. She earned it.

"Bra, bra." He heard Whiteboy say, tapping him on the shoulder with the Heineken bottle.

"Preciate it…" Ace thanked him, taking it.

Whiteboy smiled, taking a seat at Ace's side. "Man, we bout to go crazy."

"I already know," he returned. Yet he felt that would be an understatement to the hustle he planned on introducing to the streets. All sixty-six of the birds from Black's place would be stepped on with his favorite cutter, *Miami Ice*. He'd stretch it to the max then use a majority of it to acquire hitters who were willing to execute whatever and whoever for an opportunity to finally set their pockets on overload.

Ace saw the real potential in the bricks besides just serving them wholesale. Of course he'd make well over a mill that way, but he wanted to use them to produce the maximum effect. Which was to hire guns to hit Black from multiple angles, forcing him into an inevitable corner. Then, he would seize all of his clientele, assets, and connects. And then, his life, killing every bird with no more than a few moves and stones.

The ball was on his side of the court now, and he intended to score this time around. Ace laughed. How ironic was it that the very money and work Black had hustled for would end up being the same money and work to bring about his demise and the destruction of the *Hand*?

"Say, Dre..." he called out, breaking himself from his wonderful reverie. Even though he was speaking to Dre, his eyes were set on Ariel.

"Yo?"

"You still be fucking with that nigga, Tweety?"

"Hell yeah, his stupid ass. But what up?"

"Get at him. We gone need a lot of guns, right?" That was all Ace needed to say for everyone in the room to understand that shit was now real.

"AIN'T NO FUCKING WAY Y'ALL TELLING ME SOME MUTHAFUCKAS HAD the fucking balls to run up in my shit and take my shit!" Black snapped, colliding fist and palm as he paced back-and-forth in front of the group.

"Blac..." someone began but quickly got cut off.

"Man, shut the fuck up!" he growled threateningly, glaring at the individual. "Then to top it off, y'all let the muthafuckas outgun y'all... On some Wild Wild West shit and then peel the fuck out?" Black gestured with his hand at two out of the four of them.

"Now to my understanding —_nah, fuck that — I said two to three niggas in the spot at all times. So, why in the fuck wasn't two to three niggas in the spot? Explain that." He stared at Mack, one of his top soldiers and the one responsible for this particular spot —_the very important spot.

"Bl-Black..." he stuttered, intimidated by the person who held his life in his very hand. "Ma-man, we were going t..."

"Nigga..." Black stopped him. "Why the fuck wasn't you here? That's all the fuck I wanna know."

Mack lowered his head, knowing he'd fucked up by leaving the spot in the first place, and if it wasn't for Lil A getting into an altercation with some niggas, he would have been in the spot. He didn't want to leave the homie out there. Lil A was a part of the *Hand* too.

Plus, he'd been departing from it regularly for about two months now. There hadn't been any action. Better yet, there hadn't even been a fucking attempt by anybody trying anything — well, nothing before this morning. And now there wasn't one excuse he could think of that would satisfy his furious leader.

"Shhh..." Mack shook his head. "Lil A had some niggas trying to get at him, big bra. We couldn't leave 'em on stuck like that, so we went to make sure he was good."

"What? Make sure he was good?" mocked Black, like the words disgusted him. "You mean to tell me you went to get in some beef, basically saying *fuck my shit,* huh? For this childish ass lil nigga?" He finished staring at the little muthafucka who'd made room for this big ass loss. Him and Mack were next to each other, which was perfect for Black.

Mack said nothing, only shook and hung his head low. He'd fucked up.

"Oh, so this nigga that fucking important?" Black quickly pulled the snub nose .357 from behind and shot Lil A right in the stomach.

Everybody jumped away from Lil A, who stumbled backwards. His face twisted into a mix of shock and pain. He clutched the new hole in his body.

"Do something now, nigga!" Black barked provokingly, getting in Mack's face.

Digging the muzzle into his cheek, Black gritted his teeth. "I mean, this bitch was important this fucking morning. Important enough to cause me to lose over a M, nigga?"

Mack remained silent and stiff as a doorknob, grateful he hadn't received a bullet to the stomach too. Well, at least not yet.

Black kept the barrel in place another moment, becoming irritated at the sounds of distress and agony resonating from the trembling lips of Lil A. Without even glancing at him, Black fired three more rounds into him.

"Find my shit, nigga," he said it close enough to Mack's face that he smelled what he ate last night. Then, he shot Lil A again to make sure his point had gotten across.

CHAPTER TEN

"Girl, you be doing too much." Sassy chuckled, leaning up against the bathroom threshold with her arms crossed on top of her pop belly. She watched, amused, while Latoya drenched herself in MAC makeup as if she was a doll.

"What?" Latoya smiled, embarrassed. "Shoot, the way me and *Prinnnccee,*" she dragged the name out, "been kicking it for the past few days. Plus the way he treat a bitch. Girl, I'd say shit bout to get real serious." Latoya laughed, thinking of the way Prince spent money. It was like he had a tree of it.

Seriously. Sassy wondered if her best friend was for real. More than a few times, she had witnessed Latoya try the serious role with dudes who had money. And out of all those times, she'd never seen her go out of her way to impress the way she was doing now.

Hell, she really didn't have to do the extra. Her features alone were enough to make any group of dudes fight for her love. Latoya stood at 5'4" with the curves of a Coke bottle and a luscious round ass squeezed tightly under a soft coat of bronze skin. She definitely was a true object of temptation. Then, let's not forget about her shoulder length, silky hair which came from her mixed genes of Native American and Portuguese.

Latoya was a *bad bitch* in every sense of the phrase. She possessed a beauty that could easily attract another woman. Sassy even had to admit that if she hadn't been so stuck on Ace, she might have tried her best friend for a little girl on girl —_something Latoya had offered a few times before.

Sassy continued to watch her, experiencing a stab of jealousy. It was not so much because of her looks or her rendezvous with the nigga, Prince, but because she missed playing the makeup game in the mirror, prettying herself to perfection for Ace. It had been three weeks and some days since she'd seen, touched, or felt his soft lips pressed against hers. Scrolling through the pictures of him in her phone would sometimes make her feel better and at the same time cause her to miss him even more.

Baby, I miss you, she said to herself. Turning from the threshold, she hoped the love of her life could hear her words.

Grabbing the bag of Ruffle potato chips from the counter, along with some spinach cheese dip they'd ordered earlier, Sassy flopped down on the couch. That had been her usual since Latoya first started venturing off on her nightly escapades with *Prince*.

"Ughh…" mouthed Sassy, flipping through the channels as a thought of Prince intruded her mental. She couldn't put her finger on exactly what it was, but there existed something about him that she did not like. Ever since that day on the beach, she felt a weird *uneasiness*, a feeling which seemed to be giving her a real warning about this stranger. Latoya always attempted to correct her suspicion whenever she mentioned him, but damn, why was she feeling so inquietude whenever he came up as the subject?

Maybe it was the way he looked at her or the *familiar* gaze he'd given her. She could have sworn she'd seen him somewhere before, even though she had the faintest idea of where. Yet that look made her certain. She'd seen him before, and it was nowhere near South Beach.

Sassy had implored that Latoya gather as much information on him as possible. However, she'd turned up emptyhanded every single time. So, either he was good at keeping secrets or she was purposely coming up with nothing. The first tremendously heightened her suspicion.

Halting her channel search on Lifetime — her favorite — she heard Latoya finally step out of the bathroom.

"Barbie bitch or ratchet, sleazy bitch?" Latoya questioned, posing as though she was fresh off the runway.

Sassy twisted her lips. "Sleazy Barbie — bitch!" she said with a giggle.

"Uh…" Latoya paused, lifting a finger at Sassy. "Pregnant, hater bitch." She laughed before heading back into the bathroom, but she instantly stopped as a knock on the hotel's door echoed throughout the room. "Prince Charming…" She gladly smiled, pivoting and sashaying toward the door.

Looking through the peephole, Latoya saw him displaying that glamorous, Colgate smile she admired. "Yes…" She blushed from behind the door.

"Mami, how you?" Prince returned in his nonchalant demeanor.

"*Mami…*" She heard Sassy mock, making fun of the choice of word.

"Shut up," Latoya barked sotto voce as she unlocked the door.

"Welcome to Latoya's and Sassy's Inn where *most* things are possible," she gleefully said, giving her best smile to Prince, who stood before her with a bottle of Moscato. Her beaming quickly ceased after her attention drifted toward the white man who was a few feet off behind him.

Before he could get a word out, Latoya's expression changed from one of elatedness to a discomforted glare.

"Who is that?" she insisted, eyeing the guy down. Latoya wondered why in the hell Prince had brought someone to their room when she clearly told him that *nobody* was to come besides him. She seriously explained to him that Sassy had a *real* problem with strangers and had only allowed him to come because she had begged, begged, and *begged* for her to at least allow one simple visit —_which was now.

"What?!" Sassy jumped from the couch upon hearing Latoya. Now, she was in *bitch* mode, about to slam the door in both their faces. This nigga clearly didn't grasp the understanding of the *only you* part.

She slowed her steps towards the door after noticing Latoya's expression. "La…" Her name couldn't even exit her lips before Latoya began to scream.

Prince pushed his way in with the gun aimed at her face. Latoya sporadically broke away from the door.

Maneuvering with difficulty in her pregnant condition, Sassy pivoted around to reach for her purse, which sat on the side of the couch — where her Glock .26 rested. It was the same one Ace had taught her how to shoot.

Sassy crashed into the arm of the couch hard — stomach first. She ignored the pain that shot through her body and reached down into the crevice of the purse.

Hurry, Sassy! she coached herself, rambling toward the bottom, then she finally felt the steel. Coming up with it, she felt a hand grip the back of her neck, followed by a hard blow to the side of her head.

The gun slipping from her hand was the last thing she saw before the world went black.

Now, she gone be mad if I don't pick up when she call. This was the third time he'd called with no answer. It wasn't like Sassy to not pick up, especially when it was him calling. No matter what she was doing, when it came to *her baby*, she'd immediately stop, putting him before everything. But then again, she was with Latoya's crazy ass, who more than likely exhausted the shit out of his baby.

She could be more than talkative and a real busybody. But she was nothing more than a hoe with no home training at times. So, why in the fuck would he send the love of his life to South Beach with her out of all people? *What in the hell was I thinking? Stupid ass nigga.*

He chuckled at the thought and reminded himself once again that this was Latoya — the best friend who, despite all her traits and flaws, always had Sassy's best interest at heart. Their bond surpassed a mere friendship. That was why he entrusted her with his soon-to-be wife and unborn child. Besides, Sassy wouldn't have had it any other way.

Picking up the blunt from the cupholder, he snatched up the Bic lighter. "Bra, we might as well blaze. These niggas taking forever,"

Ace said to Whiteboy, who'd let his seat fall backwards and had been sitting still with his eyelids closed.

I know this nigga ain't sleep. Ace looked at him. "Shawty!" He yelled it loud as hell.

Whiteboy remained in the same position as he flatly returned, "Yeah?" from underneath the New Era fitted which laid over his face.

"Man , you always on some tired shit. Fuck is wrong with you?" Ace asked, putting the weed between his lips. Firing it up, his mind went over how much he would drop on these niggas. He wanted to acquire a couple of bands before the street war went full scale. It would definitely be at that point once Black found out who'd actually taken his shit.

His face had been off the scene for quite a while, and now, it was time to surprise everyone. But first and foremost, he needed to be smarter than his opponent — something more easily said than done. So, his mind would really have to be in full gear if he intended on ending his nemesis.

There were plenty of ways to X Black out, but he always had to rethink them and rethink them again. Black possessed a numerous amount of ways for avoiding harmful shit aimed at him. It was like he had a third eye fixated specifically for it. Therefore, whatever he plotted needed to be solid and real fuckup proof.

Black, in a sense, was like Napoleon — strategic when it came down to war and a little too arrogant for his own good. Nothing was more dangerous than an egotistical muthafucka with a band of recruits who were ready to face martyrdom in the name of his cause.

His plan would have to be the work produced by a mastermind — something he was transitioning into day by day. Ace knew the streets like the back of his hand and would use every advantage they offered meticulously.

"Nigga, is you gonna pass that?" Whiteboy asked, lifting the brim of his hat enough to see Ace.

"Shawty, you the one wit all that fake sleep shit." He took another pull then handed him the blunt. Ace glanced down at his phone. 7:24

p.m. the time read. "Man, these niggas taking forever." He pressed the call icon and placed the touchscreen to his ear.

"Yo…" Ace said into the phone. "Man, what's the hold up?" He listened, taking the blunt from Whiteboy. "Aight, keep playing. I'm bout to pull…Yeah." Before he dropped the phone back onto his lap, a call came through.

She might as well lose my number. It's over wit. He chuckled, dismissing the call from Stacey. His mind was made up already. He would renege on their deal. Once he realized that the spot belonged to Black, the shit became mandatory.

Sorry, bae, he joked, ignoring her call for the *four hundredth* time. With half the blunt gone, he dabbed the rest out. The buzz was enough. Ace never liked handling business high. However, one time he had and had also regretted every bit of it.

"About fucking time." He watched the champagne-colored Escalade in the rearview mirror as it pulled up right behind them.

They both exited, hands on their pistols. Times were hectic, and anything was possible at this point.

"What up, foo?" Woo Woo greeted them but dapped up only Ace. Whiteboy was a new face to him.

"Shit, cooling. What y'all got going on?" Ace questioned, nodding at Woo Woo's tagalong, Pat. He knew the nigga from around the way. He was another *nobody* of importance.

"Shit, man, you know a nigga just out here trying to get this bread up. Which been hard since you dipped out on a nigga. You been MIA?"

"Had to handle some outta town *b.i.* You know, nothing major though." The last thing Ace wanted was for niggas to run their mouth about anything concerning him.

"Man, please…" Woo Woo chuckled. "Nigga, it's always *something* major wit you."

"Not really," Ace returned sternly, wondering what he was getting at. Yet he didn't just want to flat out ask. "What's been up though?"

"Nothing." Apparently, Woo Woo noticed the change in his demeanor. "Shit been slow round our way. *We* been waiting on you;

things been real dry. Niggas already going elsewhere wit the fetty. Even loyal customers. So, I'm praying for you to be Jesus right now, nigga. It's dumb ugly out here."

Ace leaned against the rental's trunk casually. "I feel ya. How much bread you brought?"

"Round bout sixty."

"Nigga, that's all?" Ace joked, aware that Woo Woo wouldn't shake anything big unless he knew it was real right. He wanted only the best, which was why he refused to fuck with anybody besides Ace.

"Man, you lucky I got that much. It's been real hard on this side of the fence. A nigga almost started to fuck with the gas," he said, play punching Ace in the shoulder.

"Bra, stop all that sad shit. I got some'n real nice for you." Ace popped the trunk, retrieving an American Eagle shopping bag.

"Oh, so you gift wrapping shit now, nigga?" Woo Woo laughed as Ace handed him the bag. The work was buried under the clothes.

"Nigga, shut the fuck up. I know I can trust you, right?" Ace really didn't have to ask. Woo Woo had always kept his face clean when it came down to the money. But a reminder wouldn't hurt.

"Already know. Shid, have I ever gave you a reason not to?"

"Point. But check the move. It's six of them in there…"

"Straight up?" Woo Woo questioned incredulously. Sure, the bag had some weight, but damn!

"Fo'sho. Listen though. You gone owe me one-twenty. If you hurry and knock that off, you can give me one ten, and I'ma bless you for real on that next one."

"Say no more. Big dog, you know I got you. And how long I got?" That was the business mind of Woo Woo — always wanting to keep his business in line.

"Really like yesterday," Ace told him though knew he'd need two to three weeks. Nonetheless, he still felt it necessary to stress that time was of the essence. He had an operation to fund — Operation Dead Black.

"Say less," Woo Woo said before telling Pat to hand the money over to Ace.

Ace took the small tote bag and smiled. "We got a few more stops to make." He tossed the bag to the back.

"You ain't gonna count that?" Whiteboy asked, watching him turn over the ignition.

"For what? Niggas know what the fuck going on. Plus that's Woo Woo. He ain't gone play. It ain't in his nature," he assured him, putting the shift in drive. Then, the call came through.

Sassy. He smiled and answered. "So, when you don't pick up for me?" Instantly, his smile ceased. His mood changed as the voice on the other end spoke.

"Who the fuck is this?"

DUST FROM THE FLOORBOARD OF THE VEHICLE FLOATED — MISTED — around the small space due to the bump. The bump was what caused Sassy to stir awake.

Oh, God! Disoriented and terrified, she couldn't grasp her surroundings. A piece of tape sealed her mouth, stifling any chance of screaming. Her ability to sit up was stolen from her; her body was tightly bound to the floor of what seemed to be a van. Sassy's panicked eyes darted around, trying to make sense of the situation.

Boxes were stacked a few inches away from her head, and they were also partially out of the reach of her feet. Across from her was Latoya. She was still unconscious, strapped and gagged, exactly like her.

Sassy's stomach ached, adding more to her discomfort. She prayed her baby was fine.

She vaguely remembered what had happened — only that she had made a daring dash for her gun before everything went blank. Then, there was the glaring face of Prince, barging through their hotel door.

Why is he doing this? A tear sprang from the web of her eye. She couldn't begin to fathom why all of it had occurred. Why were they taken? Why were they strapped in like animals?

Then, Ace came to mind, causing more tears to ebb down her face.

He would surely fall apart and go crazy if he knew that this was taking place. But how would he ever find out?

Ace, baby, I need you. She spoke in her mind, attempting to imbed in her own skull that he would soon find her. Save her. She could only hope before the worst transpired. Yet wasn't her current predicament close enough to the worst?

Sassy began to fault herself, resting her head back on the vibrating metal. Damn, she knew better than to be persuaded into letting a stranger come to her room — a stranger she'd gotten too many bad vibes from.

Anxiety, hate, and anger rose within her, all of them aimed at the very person who was next to her. *If it hadn't of been for…* Her thoughts stopped briefly for a moment to rationalize. However, there was nothing to reason with in her favor. Latoya had been the reason.

The fuck was she thinking? She was now feeling like only Latoya deserved this. It was her very own lusting. It had nothing to do with Sassy — nor her unborn child. It was Latoya's own selfish thinking which led them to this baneful situation.

No! She couldn't blame her best friend. Her heart told her that Latoya would have never — in a million years — brought any harm toward her. However, she did — even if it wasn't intentional. Her recklessness was responsible.

At the same time, Sassy could have said no. But she chose to go against her own word. Now she could only pray that her, the baby, and even Latoya made it out of this predicament safely.

An hour — or perhaps hours —_passed with her lying there. Dried tear streaks marked her face. She badly wanted to escape reality, yet found it hard once her eyes opened because she was reminded of her circumstances.

Closing them back shut, she decided to focus on positive things — Ace and their future with the baby she'd birth into this world. Sassy was trying hard to prevent any negativity from invading in on her sought out destiny.

Sometime later, her eyes reopened — a lot wider than at first. The sounds of police sirens had pierced her ears.

The van slowly decreased its speed, rocking over to a stop. After hearing the tires tread over the gravel, she realized what was happening. They were being pulled over.

God, please let them hear me! she prayed. Instantly, she hummed, using every muscle in her throat to be heard. She even attempted to rock back-and-forth, but that was to no avail. The straps holding her body down were too tight and refused to allow a simple jerk.

Waiting a few moments, Sassy's ears caught nothing besides the sounds of passing traffic. She waited, trying to calm the heavy breath coming out of her nose. She needed to know if the officer had heard her pleading moans of desperation.

No luck. She could hear the officer's walkie-talkie move up the side of the van. Then, it stopped. Using everything she had, Sassy started back humming with a vengeance. It was too the point that she strained her esophagus into a violent tremble.

Quite obviously, the officer hadn't heard her muffled cries.

Please help! she begged internally as the tears piled in the corners of her eyes once again. Her endeavors were futile; nothing else could be done. She just listened.

"How are you doing, sir? You know you were traveling twenty over the limit?" the officer asked.

"Really? Well, sorry about that, but we were kinda in a hurry." Easily, she made out Prince's distinctive voice. The next words which came out stunned her to the core.

"Oh, you're an officer yourself. What city?" the officer asked, now sounding as if leniency was about to be the prescription of the day.

"Atlanta…"

Prince, a police officer? Her mind spun in circles. She found it hard to believe, even after hearing it from the horse's mouth. This new revelation caused her to try harder at provoking the officer's curiosity.

Help!!! She needed to divert his attention from their casual conversation, certainly before it ended.

Sassy's eyes had swelled a little from the previous crying. Her head slumped to the metal floor, defeated. The officer was leaving, and Prince was returning to the driver's seat of the van.

The van pulled away. She now knew they were heading toward Atlanta. Sassy was now beginning to think — and conclude — that this had been Ace's reason for telling her to leave and lay low.

The question now was: how did Prince know her and Ace? And the second one was: how did this end up being the outcome of it?

"Stop playing with it…" Black bit down on his bottom lip. His eyes locked with those of Diamond, who was squatting down between his legs, teasing his limp manhood.

"Let Mommy handle this please." She smirked seductively, sliding her tongue down the length of him, leaving behind a thin trail of saliva. Coming to the mushroom head, her mouth salivated, and then she let the ball of new spit fall onto it.

Not allowing the orb of mucus time to slide downward, her tongue scooped, flipping it back onto the head. Her soft lips consumed both.

"*Mmmmm…*" Black's head titled backwards. He wanted to grip her head, but he didn't want to fuck with this pleasure.

Twisting and pulling with her lips, Diamond squeezed the bottom of his shaft tightly, causing the tip to swell. She was determined to make him feel every bit of the sensation she was capable of bestowing.

Her head rocked from side to side ferociously. Each time his dick came out, it was accompanied by loud popping.

This can't be real. He closed one eye as his body tensed under the pressure she brought forth.

Straightening her legs, Diamond kept her hand in place, letting her ass wiggle in the air. Using her free hand, backed by her weight, she pressed down on the bottom of his stomach as hard as she could. Then, she placed her warm, moistened mouth down on him.

"Shit…" He gasped each time she took him deep into her throat. Diamond squeezed her lips tighter upon reaching the head. Like a waxed obelisk, his manhood shined with masculinity.

After a few more deep thrusts, lumps of saliva spewed from her orifice onto him. He watched as it trailed wildly.

"Girl!" Black growled, gripping the side arms of the chair, unable to focus — unbelieving that her game was this fye.

"Boyyy." Diamond giggled, running her lips up and down him. Drooling spit onto his nut sack, she smeared it with her tongue then sucked a ball into her mouth. Bobbing her head, she alternated between the two balls, massaging them one at a time. Finally twisting loose from them, Diamond took another tour over his lightening rod, leaving it drenched in her mouth's juices.

Feeling as though the job had been executed satisfactorily, Diamond smiled. Standing erect, her physique resembled that of an Egyptian goddess.

Catching his breath, Black stole a moment to admire the handiwork of the goddess then mouthed almost inaudibly, "Damn…"

The corner of her mouth creased upwards at the thought which had just sprang to mind. "Watch this." Lifting one leg, she swiveled partially sideways in a split. Then, Diamond placed her ankle on his right shoulder.

Scooting closer on one foot, she positioned her vagina directly over the top of his phallic. Both her hands found his thigh, one partly over the other.

"A little help please," she told him, rotating her hips seductively, prepping herself.

He didn't even have to think about what she meant, and he wasted no time in keeping it in place while her pussy mounted him. She slowly eased down onto him.

"Man, yo…" he began, but the warm and tight spot had engulfed him, causing the rest of his words to get caught up in his throat. Black kissed her on the calf lusciously.

She huffed a chuckle and moaned, "I know." Diamond grinded and gyrated, compressing her walls tighter around him. Each time, she tugged on his manhood as her hips lifted. Her sultry love box pulsated, releasing fluids onto him.

Diamond glanced backwards, bouncing and tugging upward in a rhythm. With her leg slightly bent, she pressed her foot against his face — something he didn't mind.

Shid, he already possessed a slick foot fetish that always gave him a hard on. Black stared at her beautiful ass as it rose and lowered, shooting a breathtaking tremor through his body

Moments later, she brought her leg down, turning a bit more while keeping him in her wetness. Diamond dropped the leg over his. "And this is the saddle." She bit down on her bottom lip, appearing sexier than ever. Forcibly, her hips came down on him, grinding hard in circular motions.

"Bitch, you fye…" he said, barely loud enough for her to hear. He gripped a palm full of ass. Damn, it was so soft. He loved it. Then, after a thought, he slid his hand to the crevice of her ass, quickly lifting it to his mouth to lubricate his middle finger. Black placed it at the top of her anal, massaging the surface.

Feeling a new touch, she arched her neck with a suggestive look. "Put it in, Daddy," she encouraged him sexually, aroused by the initiative.

Not hesitating, he let the tip penetrate her rectum. "Ooohh, baby!" Diamond moaned almost harmonically, pushing farther down on his finger and dick. "Go deeper, Daddy," she told him, digging her nails into his leg. Her muscles tensed from the building orgasm within. She was almost there.

"*Shhhiiittt!*" He dug his entire finger as deep as he could into her ass, twirling it in and out every time she rammed her pelvis against his.

"*Fffffuuucccckkkk…*" she screamed out. The more he finger fucked her, the more her ass creamed on it.

Damn, if he didn't know any better, he might have tasted it. But he wasn't turned out that much.

Trembling, her movements slowed. Diamond's ass swayed from side to side. Her vagina walls throbbed toward sensitivity. She wondered briefly if this was what a volcano experienced when it was on the verge of erupting. "Fuck! It's-bout-to-come!

"*Aghh…*" Convulsing, she bent over, nails drawing specs of blood from his thigh. Black groaned behind her. Quickly and a little weakly, she jumped off him and took him into her mouth.

Passionately, her lip's strokes caused him to collapse his hands onto her head. Within seconds, he unloaded in her throat. "Shit!" he exclaimed strongly. Black closed one eye as her head bobbed on the mushroom tip. She was attempting to suck all of it out of him.

After cleaning himself, he fired up a thick backwood, leaving Diamond Princess to shower. Black smiled a little, thinking that might have been one of the best nuts he'd caught in a while. And at the moment he was grateful for it. It had eased the tension that had been building up inside him, giving him a brief escape from the pressures weighing on his mind

Everything – lately – had been bad. Two of his spots had gotten hit, and he could think of no better way to cheer himself up besides busting a magnificent nut, something he knew his *paramour* would nonetheless guarantee.

Black blew smoke toward the ceiling, musing over how unexpected his recent misfortunes had been. Well, one of them. He pretty much figured the spot in Kirkwood was hit by no other than his former — still breathing — comrade, Ace. He understood that the occurrence was Mal delivering a message from the grave. It was one he was grateful for – somewhat. He only saw the benefit in knowing exactly what Ace's intentions could be.

A few months before Mal's fatal run in with Ace, him and Black had discussed, or better yet concluded, that a few spots needed a specific *purpose*. Like the one in Kirkwood. They weren't fools. Niggas and police alike were on the prowl, waiting on the opportunity to catch and pry information from whoever lips they'd captured.

Black knew the game and its occupants like the back of his hand. Everybody who played were capable of anything. So, likewise, the right pressure applied could make any nigga fold and turn coat. That was part of the game. And he saw it for what it was. He only wanted to lessen its detriment or loss.

You couldn't avoid the losses, he knew. It came with life. You could only do the next best thing, and that was to try keeping it at a minimum. That was Black's goal. However, he was very aware of the fact that attempting to prevent it period would result in an even bigger loss.

So, spots, like the one in Kirkwood, were designated for *that* purpose. For losses. It allowed him to grasp an understanding of exactly what he'd be dealing with.

However, the Kirkwood hit had still caught him off guard a little, along with Ace's little disappearing act. It had been the smallest one on the list and the most vulnerable. But Black was certain he'd go for the main two —_the two he'd organized to the tee. If a nigga decided to run off in either of them, he wouldn't make it out – let alone in one piece. Even if a band of troops were to aid in the campaign, they'd encounter the same fate.

He guessed Ace was trying to play it smart by exercising good judgement, while easing his way up the ladder. There wasn't any doubt about Ace going for the other two. Vengeance was set in his heart. Murder – he knew – would also remain at the forefront of his mind. Black saw this as a good thing. Ace's anger would bind him in Black's snares – like the cheese waiting patiently in the trap for the greediest mouse.

And Black was definitely waiting.

Then, there was his main house, perfectly ducked off in a hidden part of Clayton County. Only a few knew about it — and those particular people had no idea what really laid within it.

Yet two of his top lieutenants had knowledge of it – one of which was killed, the other under close scrutiny. It didn't take a rocket scientist to know that D had told about what laid up in the ceiling. He could almost understand. D had been brutally tortured then stabbed to death.

Black cared less about him dying though. D could be replaced. His dope and those responsible were of the upmost importance. If you asked for his honest opinion, he'd say the hit seemed too much like an inside job. It went like clockwork.

First, niggas were out of pocket when they should have been present. D was by himself, and somehow, people managed to get in without kicking the fucking door down. This was the biggest mystery. D knew better than to let anyone besides the *Hand* in. And D was very loyal, so Black couldn't see him doing such.

However, they somehow got in and went directly for what their minds were set on. They even had enough time to back a van up in the driveway, load up sixty-six bricks. Seventy-two were left, and had it not been for Swift, all seventy-two would have landed in the hands of the *real police*. Then to top it off, they executed a real Wild Wild West shootout with the aid of some hoe who Black planned on putting a face on before they did away with his shit.

His instincts told him to lay all the fault at Mack's doorstep, something he still intended on doing. But it would have to wait – at least until he found out exactly who had his work.

Black now felt the urge to laugh, thinking about how these clown ass niggas had ripped off pieces of a bed sheet to cover their faces. This caused him to assume that the intruders were more than mere strangers. They were *someone*s they knew. Had to be. What else could explain it? By the way it all played out, it was obvious that they didn't plan on niggas showing up. They were forced to improvise to keep their true identities hidden. Damn, but D would know.

Eventually though, he'd find out. No one could move that much work without someone running their mouths. All he needed to do was let the inevitable run its course.

Taking another drag from the blunt, his eyes followed Diamond as she sauntered across the carpet with a towel wrapped around her blessed frame.

She was truly a piece of Heaven – a fresh breath of life.

His phone began to emit its tune loudly. "Run ya mouth…" he answered, keeping his retinas on the work of art.

"Nothing…" he said after a moment. "Did you find my shit?" Black let the smoke escape his nose. Diamond was now on the bed spread eagle, applying baby oil to her voluptuous physique.

"Oh, yeah?" He sounded partially surprised, causing Diamond to seek his undivided attention again. Gazing backwards, she began to tease him by rubbing the oil sexily between her round ass cheeks.

"When?" Black gripped his dick, ready again. "Aight, the shit better be exact."

Letting his thumb slide over the red icon, he ended the call. He took one step, about to toss the phone to the chair, when another call came through.

The contact name appeared on the screen, causing his body to stiffen. His jawbone clenched, not believing that this muthafucka actually had the audacity to call him.

"Fuck nigga, really?" he growled.

"Fuck!" Ace yelled, slamming a fist into the steering wheel after trying to make contact with Stacey. The last attempt had been the twentieth.

"I'ma kill this bitch. I swear. Man, they betta not hurt her…" Ace barked, unable to control himself. Damn, he wanted to kill somebody —_a particular somebody. Rage pumped furiously through his veins. His blood pressure surged through the roof, and his sugar was on the floor.

They had somehow found and kidnapped the only person who made a real difference in his world, the one who exuded an unconditional love for him, the same one who carried his seed.

How could I let this happen? he asked himself repeatedly before finally dropping his head against the steering wheel. Ace was supposed to be the one to keep her safe — out of harm's way. And now staring reality in the face, it was evident that he'd failed tremendously.

His entire reason for sending Sassy out of town had been to keep her and their unborn clear of the mess that he was making. At this very moment though, it seemed as if he'd thrown her right into the sinking ship.

He now faulted himself for being so stupid and reckless, for reneging on Stacey and her people — people who quite obviously had their eyes set on Sassy before she even left.

Ace was aware that Stacey had knowledge of his girl, yet not on a convo or seeing basis. But she stayed in the lofts — on the same hall —_mere doors away from where he first met her

Thinking about the simple encounter, he remembered how he'd foolishly made mention of *his girl* when they were in the elevator.

He had exposed his very weakness — his heart. He wanted so badly to hand over to her — or her people —_the entire take from Black's spot. Right now, he would give whatever was necessary to get the love of his life back.

Now Stacey wasn't answering the phone, ignoring him, exactly like he'd previously done a week and some hours ago.

"Fuck!" he shouted again. He'd fucked up big time.

"Bro…" Whiteboy finally said something. "Chill, we gone get her back." He could tell Ace was on the verge of breaking down. That glossy glow of redness took over the white of Ace's eyes. Whiteboy wanted to feel his pain, so he could fully understand what he was going through at this moment. But he couldn't. He only had love for the person who sat across from him.

"Chill?" Ace glared at him. "Nigga, how the fuck I'ma chill? Nigga, how bout you have the only muthafucka you care about taken from you? Then you tell yourself to chill, nigga!"

"I did…" Whiteboy flatly returned, unaffected by his best friend's words. Had the situation been different, he might have felt some type of way. Whiteboy vehemently remembered experiencing what Ace was feeling right now. That was how he felt when they took him away from the only friend he knew.

Ace went silent instantly. He read between the lines in Whiteboy's remark. However, that still wouldn't change anything. She wasn't just another nigga he'd ran with in the streets. Sassy was his universe and pregnant with their world. That was something Whiteboy wasn't, so how could he compare the situations?

"White, ma…" Ace shook his head, finding it hard to finish what he was about to say. He turned his face toward the ceiling. Ace prayed that God would send him some type of sign that meant she'd be okay and would make it out of this shit unharmed.

A tear formed in the corner of his eye as he heard the vehicle's door click open for Whiteboy to spit.

"Shawty, my word, we gonna get her back…" Whiteboy assured him. It was either that or they'd body the city together.

"We-we got to. Bra, I can't live without her," was all he could say.

He then picked his phone up. He called the number he knew all too well. Ace figured *his* hands could have already been in it. And if not, at least he'd help find out where she was, especially if he wanted his work back.

"Fuck nigga, really?" Black answered.

At first, Ace didn't know what to say. The last time they talked, he told him that he was going to kill him. He was still more than ready to do it and take everything he had, but as of right now, he desperately needed help.

"Black…" he uttered his name as if pronouncing it had put a very bad taste in his mouth. "I ne…" Damn, he had to put his pride to the side. "I need ya help. They got her." He straight out told him. There was no reason to beat around the bush. Plus, what else would these two have to talk about? The damage had already been done.

Black chuckled incredulously. "You need my help? Nigga, you got some fucking nerves calling me — out of all people — for some muthafucking help. I wouldn't help if my life depended on it. Fuck you!" Then, the call ended.

Ace expected that and hated himself for having to call him back. But he couldn't afford to be stubborn — definitely not at a time like this —with Sassy in her current predicament. He called again.

Black answered on the second ring, this time yelling. "Nigga, find…"

"Shut the fuck up and listen if you want your shit back," Ace scolded into the phone. With that being said, he now had Black's full attention, though he glanced at the phone to make sure that he hadn't hung up. The timer was still ticking away.

"Some people took Sassy because of them fucking bricks…"

Who?" Black quickly asked, not allowing him enough time to finish. He was finding it hard to accept that whoever he was talking about would do that unless… Black smiled. It was becoming clear.

"I don't know, but they want the work *I got* for her. Have you ran into a bitch named Stacey?" Ace knew Black probably only heard the part about him having his dope. Which he cared less about at this moment. It was what it was.

Black remained silent a few seconds, letting Ace continue. "She's a mid-height, dark-skinned chick, playing like she's a college student or some shit." Ace thought better of it to give him a little more to go off of. There was no telling who this hoe actually was.

"Hold on," Black returned, thinking about the name and description. He knew a few *Staceys* but only one in particular fit the description perfectly.

Were they that stupid? Things were clearing up by the second. Finally, Black said, "Nah…" Of course he knew her, yet he needed to keep Ace in the blind and talking. At this point, he knew Ace would continue to tell it all until the pieces of the puzzle fell into place. "But what this hoe got to do with my shit and Sassy?"

Ace had already prepared himself for this question. He just hated that the circumstances wouldn't allow him to enjoy Black's reaction. "Nigga, she the one who put me on your spot. Like, you do this and this a happen. Ain know who shit it was at first, then I came across D…" He lied at the end. The clock was ticking, and he didn't have time for the extra shit.

"So, you knew *then* and still took my shit? Letting D soak in his own blood?"

For good reason, this brought a semi-smile to Ace's face. "Man, that shit is what it is. Nigga, you know what the fuck going on."

"And yo bitch ass need my help now, lil nigga."

"*And* you want your shit, pussy nigga," Ace grumbled, making the disrespect and situation mutual. He had to remind him that they both had *wants* in this shit.

Black offered a half-hearted laugh. "I guess." He found it amusing that Ace thought he could hold the work over his head. Black added it to the pile of mistakes that little Ace would die for after he got what was rightfully his. "Aight, let me holla at some people and I'ma hit you when I know everything."

"Cool, just remember that time is of the essence, Black," Ace told him before disconnecting the call.

. . .

Black stared at the screen of his phone, musing over all the things he'd just caught wind of. It was all a big surprise. The mutha-fuckas had plotted and executed their grand scheme, most likely thinking it wouldn't find his ears.

There were more questions though which needed to be answered, and it would only be a matter of time before he got all those answers.

Agents Swift and White were the puppet masters, orchestrating this entire mess. He could see how setting it all up would benefit them. They were trying to fix the big mess they had already made — the mess they probably thought he hadn't heard about.

Lost in thought, Black moved away from the bed and stared out of the window. He became mad at himself for thinking he could trust someone with *his* type of credentials. It had been four years of them working together. Secretly, Swift had worked for him, and in return, Black provided him with various sums of cash.

Also, more than a few times, Black had given him information to pass on to his supervisors, so Swift could make a few *good* busts, which would keep him assigned to the Atlanta division. As well, Swift in return gave him the drop on local hustlers, who he'd strip if they were making noise.

It had been a loyal relationship. Hell, the best relationship because they were both making big paper. Up until now.

For some strange reason, the affair with Reno came to the front of his mind. He now wondered whether the shit with Reno was even what Swift said it was. Or had there been something more that led him to push the issue of getting rid of Reno versus his talking a little too much about *detrimental factors*. Swift told him that Reno's words could end them both — though more like ending him.

Shit was getting out of hand. Black would have to bag and bury it quickly before any more *out of hand* occurrences took place.

"Say, Pee Pee..." Black spoke into his phone, pivoting away from the window. "Meet me in thirty at Lenox."

All of this was about to end, he determined, starting with the death of the agents. But not before Ace.

CHAPTER ELEVEN

Tossing and turning, Ace was unable to get any type of sleep —_period. He laid there motionless, worrying himself to death about Sassy. How was she doing? Was she hurt? Was his unborn okay? These questions were the only ones to occupy his mind for the past few days.

And they had been the worst three days of his life. He felt like he was dying on the inside without her. He pleaded with God just to hear her say a simple, "I love you."

Only if he knew where she were. Nothing would stop him from going to her, killing any and everybody who had anything to do with it. Whatever he had to do, he would. He desperately needed to feel her — smell her.

The first night was hell. He cried wildly, clutching and angrily waving the pistol, wishing he had a target —_anyone to unload on. A thought crossed his mind about how to go out and release some of his tension on the first person he saw. *But what would that do?*

Ace rolled on his side, facing the nightstand, checking the time on his phone. *10:12 p.m.*

Finally, he dragged his body from the covers, going straight for the bathroom. Ace turned on the hot water then stared at his defeated reflection in the mirror. Steam rose between his face and the reflector, distorting this horrible image.

He looked mentally ill, like someone who was falling deeper into the abyss of depression, like he was in serious need of medication. And he definitely was. Ace dipped his head toward the water, splashing his face. Maybe this would help remove the lifelessness from his ashen skin.

The water felt good cascading down his face. It eased some of the tension which had settled into his features. Now all he needed was something to take away the misery and anxiety that rode the highway of his soul — something the water couldn't wash away.

Ace splashed his face a couple more times before shutting it off and boring into himself. He swiped his hand across the condensation for a better look.

"Shhh…" he lowly let out, letting his eyes fall into the depth of the drain. At this very moment, his life resembled it — a vessel used for life to run through until it was finally left empty.

The exhausted reflection begged for his attention again. He needed to grasp all that he'd caused.

"Shit!" He jerked backwards, startled — though not by himself but by the brief appearance of Missy.

Ace rubbed his eyes, thinking that he was losing it. This had been similar to the minute mirage in the mall. Another flash sighting of his mother, who lay dying in the hospital.

"Missy," he said softly, praying that he wouldn't lose her as well. It had been a while since he last visited her. So much had transpired between then and now. Shamefully, he now realized that he hadn't even allowed a simple thought of her to come forth.

He would now.

STEPPING OFF OF THE ELEVATOR, THE NAUSEATING SMELL OF ILLNESS rushed into his nostrils with a vengeance. Ace hated the way hospitals reeked of disease and death. The scent never changed — only the patients did. He silently prayed. He didn't want to become one of its occupants. He would rather die before it came to suffering like this.

Ace moved along the corridor, stepping past the victims of life's calamities, who were waiting on death to open its door. Some though, he could tell were dearly hanging on to that last string of life for reasons only they knew.

I'd rather just be done with it, he thought, gazing at one patient who was hooked up to tubes and machines. The man's eyes were barely open.

Again, he'd prefer to die in the streets than in a hospital's gallery where you were exposed, basically put on display. Like you were for all passing spectators to make small talk about the gruesome scene which left an imprint on their mental.

Six-twelve, the plaque that was situated above the door he now stood in front of read. Ace took a deep breath, actually glad he'd made the decision to come here. She was another person in the world who loved him unconditionally.

The TVs fluorescence was the only lighting in the dim room. He began to wonder if she was asleep. The timing was late, and if she was asleep, it wouldn't matter. He just wanted to see her.

Strolling past the first bed where an elderly woman slept, he eased the curtain to the side. He was shocked to find Missy's wide eyes staring at him as if she'd been waiting. The sight scared the hell out of him.

She looked like she was possessed. Then, she smiled. "Hey, baby, how have you been?"

Ace leaned in to give her a hug. "Alright. How you, Ma?" he asked, gazing down at his mother, who seemed to be aging a little too fast. Clearly the threatening disease wasn't letting her go.

Her dried lips cracked open farther. "I'm good, just waiting on that big day…"

He mustered a smile. "Well, you gonna wait a long time." Ace hated seeing her in this condition. Yet he loved the way she accepted and strode with it.

"So, where's that grandbaby of mines?" she asked, reminding him of his promise to her.

With those particular words, Ace dropped his head. He honestly didn't know what to tell her. But he refused to tell her the truth. The last thing he wanted was to add more stress and pain to the suffering she was already experiencing.

Forcing a light smile to stay on his lips, Ace lifted his face back up, though a nerve had been hit.

"He isn't here yet, Missy." He almost choked as he tried hard to hold back the tears which desperately wanted to spring themselves free.

"Oh…Well, how long is she due? I can't leave without seeing him."

"Another two months." On the outside, he managed to remain intact. But on the inside, he had already crumbled.

"Another t…" She paused. Missy knew her son all too well. She could see that something weighed heavily on his mind. His eyes said it all. "Ace, baby, what's wrong?"

"Nothing, Ma," he quickly returned, knowing she'd see through the fake act. She had always been able to.

"Ace, I know it's more than *nothing*. You haven't called me *Ma* since you were five," she said with a stoic expression.

She had made him, he realized. Yet he still couldn't bring himself to tell her.

"Is it the baby or the girl?" Her expression now switched to one of concern.

After another silent moment, he attempted to assure her. "Everything okay, Missy, everythi…" He couldn't even get the rest out. Tears began to pore from the webs of his eyes, streaming sporadically down his face.

"Come here…" she said, sitting all the way up. Missy rubbed his head as her shoulders became his pillow.

"It's okay, baby. It'll be okay." She decided to let him keep whatever it was to himself. Ace was a man, and he'd have to deal with it like one. Hearing it wouldn't make her better, but it would cause him to fall deeper into an emotional state — something she didn't want because she knew that alone would bring him more harm than good. She needed for him to be strong.

"Ace…" She started back, lifting his face to hers. "Whatever it is, I know you gonna fix it. You too strong not to…"

His mother's words encouraged him a little. They even helped a little, just not as much as her shoulder had done. It was the one thing he had needed.

"THERE THAT NIGGA ASS RIGHT THERE," DRE MUTTERED AS HE SAT IN the driver's seat of the Denali with Whiteboy riding shotgun.

The two had been sitting in the parking lot of East Hampton apartments for a little over three hours now. They sat less than a few feet away from the very first *spot* Ace had taken him to.

Tonight though, him and Dre were here for more than a mere visit. Whiteboy had come up with an idea — the exact same one they were about to execute in a few minutes. Hopefully.

Whiteboy couldn't stand sitting around watching Ace stress over the kidnapping of his baby's mother. It was breaking his best friend by the day. And it irked him day by day. He couldn't sit around anymore and not do anything.

Ace, he noticed from the last time he'd seen him, which was two days ago, was a fucking wreck. He had never seen any nigga under such misery and agony like Ace exuded. And Whiteboy didn't want to make logic out of what was going on in his mind. He just wanted his friend back.

It made him furious to see his brother in such a distressed state — like a man with no hope besides that of a barrel in his mouth, his very own fingers playing teasingly to the tune of death.

Niggas would die until she was back in his arms. Until his best friend was Ace again. At the moment, no other thoughts invaded his mental. Nothing but the accomplishment of those objectives.

And this was the starting place. Fuck where it would end.

Whiteboy watched the guy throw a hand up, uttering some last words to a group of dudes standing in the building's hallway.

As the dude began to pull out, Dre turned over the ignition, keeping the headlights off. They waited a couple of seconds then took the same route as their prey.

Making a left out of the parking lot, Dre kept a distance between them, easing the SUV up the hill casually. He slowed behind their target as they approached a red light.

Whiteboy could tell by the movement of his silhouette that he was obviously enjoying himself on the phone, too oblivious of how things were about to take a drastic turn for him.

"Now…" Whiteboy said to Dre, going against the original plan, which was to wait until he turned on a vacant street. Then, they would intentionally bump into the back of him as if it had been an accident. Once he got out to view the damage, they'd snatch him up.

However, at this very moment, Whiteboy felt the perfect opportunity had showed its face, even with the gas station's brightly lit lights. No one would expect something so bold.

A few people were at the gas station to their right, minding their own business. Only some drunks, along with a couple of crack heads, sat on the walls. Some were in small groups, doing their usual — waiting on another chance to get high.

Before letting his foot off of the brakes, Dre glanced over at Whiteboy, making sure this was where he wanted to do it at. Whiteboy must of seen something that he hadn't.

The Denali inched forward, ramming into the rear of the Challenger, causing a crashing sound to resonate a tad louder than they intended it to.

The guy driving the Challenger jerked toward the steering wheel from the impact. Immediately, he went into a frenzy, mouth clapping as he wildly pointed in all directions. Apparently, he was cursing them the fuck out. His head moved comically as he maneuvered the vehicle onto the gas station parking lot.

"Damn, he didn't get out," Dre said, turning in behind him.

"Fuck it. We gone do it right here. Fuck these people," Whiteboy returned, snatching back the slide on the Glock nine.

"Under all these lights? Nigga, you shell." Dre could already tell he was dead ass serious. He only wished that he would have stuck to the original plan because, surely, there'd be a good bit of onlookers when shit got to popping off. In no time, DeKalb County police would be alerted and on the way.

Parking directly behind the Challenger, Dre was out first, quickly pretending to be shocked while examining the small-scale damage. The truck's bumper was hanging some, but he didn't give a fuck about it. It had been stolen for this purpose.

Just as quick, dude jumped out.

"Fuck!" he exclaimed dramatically, phone still in hand. He glared at Dre with a look that said, "Had this happened at any other place, you'd be begging for yo life, nigga."

"Damn, my nigga. My bad…" Dre lifted his palms up innocently then continued. "Shid, look, my bad bout that, shawty. I'll cover it, no matter the cost. But let's leave twelve out of this. A nigga looking real bad on the Ls, feel me?" With that, Dre pulled a wad of cash out. His ear caught the almost inaudible sound of the door clicking open.

"Shawty, yen even got that much. This a muthafucking 2018 in case ya didn't notice," the guy aggressively returned, evidently fronting for whoever was on the other end of his phone.

Keeping to the script, Dre pretended to be intimidated as he cowered a few steps backwards. "Well, shid, I got some more bread right here…" He nodded toward the Denali for him to have a look.

Stupidly, the dude went for it. Dre couldn't believe he was so simple minded. He wondered where all the niggas with street sense had gone. Clearly, they were becoming extinct.

After he took a couple more steps in Dre's direction, he halted after seeing a shadow move at the rear of the truck. Dude had to thank the gas station's luminous lights because without them, he might have missed whoever it was.

"The fuck type sh…" His words trailed off as he reached for his strap.

Dre hadn't seen the alarmed movement because he was still in his role, pulling open the driver's door. Yet Whiteboy had, where upon he quickly sprang from the rear, gun aiming.

"Nigga!" he shouted right before firing two rounds.

One of the slugs launched into dude's side while he was in the process of turning. The second one missed by an inch.

"Bitch…" the guy yelped, wasting no time in fleeing. He fired back recklessly.

"Get the truck!" Whiteboy yelled over his shoulder, in pursuit of the dude who dodged across the four-way intersection. Whiteboy ran, watching cars screech to swerving stops, trying to avoid hitting the person who scrambled like death was the linebacker chasing him.

Without a steady shot, Whiteboy sent another round his way, knowing that he'd miss. But it was still worth the try to him.

As if making it to the end zone, the man stepped onto another gas station's lot. He slowed down, attempting to measure the damage done. The bullet was taking effect on his physical, forcing his scamper to fall into a desperate hop. The people — he noticed — were frighteningly clearing out of his way, some jumping into their vehicles, others taking cover behind their cars. He turned, aimed, and saw no one.

Thinking that he'd escaped his pursuer, he slowed his strut even more. He assumed dude had given up due to all the publicity. His hand clutched his side.

"Muthafu…" he grumbled, frantically attempting to make it into the Phillips 66, so he could at least stash the pistol before the police showed up. A convicted felon with a gun wouldn't be a good look, regardless of his crippling circumstances.

He kept switching his gaze from the front to the back of him. Paranoia was definitely starting to take its toll on him. This shit had fucked up his night.

The sound of sliding tires caused him to abruptly swivel around. The SUV which hit his car had swerved into the parking lot.

Fuck! He was in the act of raising the gun toward the truck when, out of nowhere, someone slammed into him from the side, sending him flying to the pavement. The gun flew from his grasp.

Hurriedly, Whiteboy kicked the gun even farther away. "Bitch ass nigga!" he scolded, smacking him in the face with his gun.

The Denali stopped directly behind them. Snatching him up by his neck, Whiteboy forced him into the backseat, snuggling in beside him. The door was still open as the truck pulled away.

"Hoe ass nigga!" Whiteboy angrily snapped, bashing him two more times with the pistol.

Pee Pee's world slowly faded into darkness as the tunes of sirens blared at a distance.

THE ROOM WAS DARK, REEKING OF URINE, MOLD, AND FECES. IT WAS IN the middle of summer. This meant that the stench was smoldering, causing the atmosphere in the small space to be one of miasma.

No light occupied or entered the room unless the door opened, letting in the radiant glow from the hallway. This — to them — was the closest thing to daylight, but what time of day though?

This dreadful isolated cell of darkness had been Sassy and Latoya's abode for God knows how many days now. Sassy had lost track of time after they were removed from the van with clothes being placed over their heads.

She attempted to keep up with it by logging each time portions of food came through the threshold. But quickly that proved to be irregular. *Or was it?* She wasn't for sure.

Drenched in her very own body fluids, she felt disgusted, beaten, and wretched. Sassy imagined dying in this room, becoming a quick add on to its already gruesome nature.

She was certain somebody had died in it before. The grim aroma told her so. Lord knows how many times this place — this room — had been used for exactly what it was being used for now — to house the slowly deteriorating.

Thoughts of her future began to fade, along with all her hopes and prayers. Everything was gone besides that fatal action which would cause her demise — something she now embraced as inevitable.

Her stomach ached so bad — for so long — that she became almost immune to the pain. She could only think about the types of conditions her baby was suffering, which probably wouldn't matter in the end.

She'd die, and her unborn would face the same fate inside of her. However, Sassy took a little pleasure in knowing that the baby was of no conscious, so it wouldn't experience the severity of dying. *Damn, what kind of God would allow this? What kind of God have I been praying to?* She could only wonder.

Then, what about her Ace? He had already exited her mentality. She accepted the fact that he'd never be able to find her — to save her. It hurt her deeply to know she'd never again get a chance to say a simple "I love you" to him. Two fucking unpretentious words, proceeded by a single letter.

A hopeless tear slid from the web of her eye. She knew he'd continue to search, only to never find her. They were each other's life's — *lives*. Their love couldn't be broken, but their future was on the verge of being shattered into pieces — pieces never to be found, never to be put together again.

God, why? Sassy wanted to cry out through her dry lips. Why and how could a thing so perfect be ripped into shambles by the evil hands of man? What had she done so wrong to deserve this? What had the love of her life done?

At times, she wanted to blame him for all of it. All of this. For their life being suddenly torn apart. For her current predicament. Yet her love for him was too great to even allow the negative thought to manifest within her mind.

He was everything to her. Her forever more. And nothing would change that. Regardless of the situation, Sassy would, nonetheless, love him absolutely. She'd die madly in love with her Ace.

She stared into the unpiercing darkness, toward the direction she last saw Latoya in. Sassy wanted to know at this very moment what her thoughts and feelings were. Badly, she needed to talk to her best friend.

After many attempts of whispering when the cloth wasn't over her mouth, she got nothing in return. Not even a moan or whimper. She felt as though her bestie had already exited mentally.

But physically, she could tell that she was still alive. The last time food came, Sassy locked eyes with Latoya, who blankly stared back. Her eyes were glossy and lifeless. Just like those of a zombie. She had barely eaten more than a few spoonsful. Quite clearly, this harsh reality was taking its toll on her. The house —_this room — was eating at her soul. Hell, both of theirs. Gulping big chunks with every passing minute. Because of her own doing.

However, Sassy wanted to let her know that it wasn't her fault. That maybe — somehow — they'd get through this, even if she didn't believe it herself.

She dropped her head, prepared and ready for all of it to finally end. Then, the door clicked open.

The rays of light appeared to be a bit duller than they had been before. More gloomy — or maybe it was just her imagination. Nothing about life seemed bright anymore.

Sassy's retinas immediately jolted toward her best friend, who remained in the same position as before —_slumped in the abyss of hopelessness.

A darkened figure entered, stepping in front of Sassy, who might have cringed backwards in fear if her body was able to do so.

He began to fish something from his pocket. It was a cell phone. He was making a call when the second person entered the room. This one had stopped mere inches away from Latoya.

What's going on? She couldn't help but to wonder as she caught ear of the faint voice on the other end of the phone. The individual then placed the phone to the side of her face.

"Why are you doing this?" she asked, ignoring the phone until it was pressed harder against her face. "Hello? Who is this?" she asked, frightened and bewildered.

Then, she heard the last voice in the world she expected to hear. "Ace…" she coughed. Her heart skipped a beat as a wave of shock and hope — joy — shot through her body. But she refused to let the opportunity be stolen by the sudden surprise.

Seizing the opportunity, she yelled, "It's the police, Ace!" Just as quick as she had said it, a hand struck her across the face.

Angered with newfound adrenaline — new hope — she spit on the perpetrator.

BOOM!!!

The loud gunshot resonated throughout the small area, causing Sassy to freeze in horror. Every muscle in her throat became stiff, denying her sound. The world stopped.

Her eyes mooned at the sight of Latoya's cranium slumping backwards. Reality suddenly set back in.

Tears instantly shot from her eyes. She stared at her lifeless friend. "Noooo, *Latoya!!!*"

"Sassy!" Ace yelled into his phone. The sound was unmistakable. His heart fell though not to the pit of his stomach as it should've. The call ended with the laughter of the kidnapper and Sassy's cries in the background. She wasn't the one to take the bullet, though she witnessed the death of her best friend.

"Oh, fuck," he gasped through trembling lips, staring at his phone unbelievingly.

Ace turned his gaze back to his mother, who looked as if she understood it all now. Though she said nothing. The silence seemed to work better than any words she could muster.

Fury began to rage from the depths of him internally. His jaws clenched tighter as his facial features distorted into a sculpture of death. He wanted to kill. He was in need of blood — all because she desperately needed him.

His eyes swept again to the phone. *"It's the police."* Her words rang loudly inside of his head now. *The police? How and why was they involved? Why would they kidnap her?*

Questions and thoughts wrestled wildly throughout his mental, making it unbearable for him to even find a place to start in sorting them out. And his anger made it no better.

Ace needed some *alone* time — enough to at least sort half of his problems out. Shit had got even realer.

"Missy…" he began but another call came through. "Yeah…" he reluctantly answered.

"Shawty, where you at?" Whiteboy asked.

"At the hospital…" He shook his head, trying not to let any emotion ride his voice. "Man, them m…" He caught himself. Ace wanted to tell Whiteboy about the call, but he remembered who he was in the room with. Though what exactly did he have to hide? Missy came from the heart of the streets, so she had most likely already put it all together.

However, he still wouldn't allow himself to be the reason her condition worsened. Nor the reason stress weighed more heavily on her heart.

"Hol up…" he spoke into the phone, staring at Missy, whose expression said she understood. "I love you, Missy, and I'ma make it better," he assured her. He would, or he would die trying.

She reached, kissing him on the forehead like she used to do when he was her little boy. "I know you will. You Ace."

With that, he stepped into the hallway, quickly moving for the elevators.

"Man, White, they just hit me. Shawty, they…" He had to catch himself. A ton of nausea began to pile itself at the front of his head. He had to keep his composure — or fall apart, making matters worse. "They deaded her friend in front of her," he snarled lowly.

"Damn…" was all Whiteboy could return. He knew what this shit was doing to his brother from another mother. "Man, we gone clap everybody till she returns. That's my muthafucking word."

Ace's mind's state had already reached that point. He only needed a direction — a list of targets to be exact.

"And right now," Whiteboy continued, "I got the first muthafucka we starting wit." He glared downward, kicking the tied up Pee Pee, bringing a muffled groan from him.

They ended the call after Whiteboy relayed their whereabouts. Ace hadn't the slightest clue as to who he'd abducted or why. But he didn't give a damn. Anybody could get it. And anybody would.

. . .

FINALLY, HE MADE IT OUT TO COLLEGE PARK, AT THE DEPOT Whiteboy had designated as their location. Darkness veiled a lot of the landscape, leaving nothing besides that of an antique warehouse to stand out like a sore thumb.

Ace stepped out of the rental, gazing over at the SUV his protégés were driving. The building looked abandoned with old train tracks penetrating the bottom of its walls.

His eyes swept over the deserted area, wondering whose fate would be decided in such a forsaken place — one which probably hadn't been visited in years.

Quickly, he noticed that the large steel doors in the front of the building were chained shut. He pulled out his phone, about to call Whiteboy, until a voice spoke. "Say…"

His head snapped in the direction it had come from, where upon he saw the dark silhouette of Dre's physique at the edge of the structure. Ace proceeded in his direction, dapping Dre before he tugged him closer in a hug like manner.

"You good?"

"Yeah," Ace returned, thankful for his concern. But he didn't need anybody's sympathy — just somebody's blood and life.

Following Dre, he could see Whiteboy at a short distance, standing almost under the light pole. Ace glanced around, wondering why in the hell there was one light pole there and nowhere else as far as he could tell.

His ear caught a few hard to make out words, obviously coming from White, who pointed down at their captured.

Pee Pee. He smirked upon getting closer. What a surprise. Pee Pee was the one to lead the assault on the spot where a bullet had grazed him. Well, more like scratched him.

And now, thinking about it, Ace's jaw clenched. "What's popping, lil bitch?" he growled, kicking him where his hand was covering his injury.

"Agh, fuck!" Pee Pee tried to recoil from the agonizing blow.

Ace knelt down, glad to see the terror in the depths of his eyes. "Now, I wonder what in the hell could you say to save yo life?"

Pee Pee glanced up at him with blood and dirt heaped together on the side of his face. He knew Ace and understood the situation perfectly. There was nothing — not even a simple fucking prayer — he could utter which would guarantee he'd live beyond tonight. He accepted his fate.

"Nothing?" Ace's lips spread into a smile. His facial features became that of a crazy individual. He removed the Ruger from his waist.

"Yeah…" Pee Pee finally mumbled, thinking his next words would surely put the nail in his coffin. Yet to him, they'd be well worth it.

"Okay." Ace rotated his hand with the pistol, as if to say, *Let's do it*.

The corner of Pee Pee's mouth creased upwards. "Fuck you and die slow. You and that pregnant bitch." His head laid back onto the dirt. He was welcoming the inevitable.

Whiteboy swiftly moved closer, about to make him eat those words. Ace stopped him, putting his hand up.

Ace stared at Pee Pee. The words from his mouth continued to vibrate through the blood of his veins until they penetrated his core.

This vulnerable nigga — he realized — knew he'd die when they snatched him up. So, there was nothing he could execute to make him regret every syllable he had pronounced. He had already been shot and most likely tortured at some point — all of which left him knocking at death's door. Ace wished he was in better shape.

His emotions flared some though, burning his mind into an unknown calm state. It was a foreign one but also an acceptable one. At this very moment, his feelings would die along with Pee Pee. He'd give all hell till he reached it.

Ace leveled the muzzle with Pee Pee's chest, sending two slugs into his torso and one toward his skull. Then, he smirked as he watched his body slump over on its back. His life began to shiver away.

"Die slow…" Ace said, almost in a whisper, before he walked away.

Making it back to the front, Ace instructed them to blaze the truck. A thought ran across his mind.

"Shid, I already wiped it down," Dre told him. He was aware that they'd have to leave with him. They'd be taking too much of a big risk driving it again, especially after what they'd done at the gas stations.

"I want them to find him. This way, Black a know shit is serious and that more of his own will die till shit was fixed. Now light that muthafucka." His demeanor transformed into something other than their leader. Dre and Whiteboy could see it in Ace's eyes that he'd been replaced by none other than the devil himself.

After stuffing a piece of shirt into the gas tank, Dre lit the tip then backpedaled toward the rental.

They pulled away as the truck blew, lighting up the scenery like the Fourth of July.

CHAPTER TWELVE

It was eight thirty in the morning. Ace had been up since five o'clock, trying with everything in him not to think about Sassy.

He sat on the couch, staring off into space. He was lost in a realm which was better than the one he suffered, the one he wished to exit if he couldn't have her.

His body remained stiff as a doorknob with only the thoughts within his head in motion. He leaned back into the past, vehemently recalling the first misunderstanding between him and Black and the encounter with Sassy. Memories flashed from their first meeting to the intimate moments then culminated in the haunting recollection of a dark event — when he had taken the lives of his father, brothers, and sister.

Too much had occurred. Too many niggas had died, and some had switched sides. Missy was ill. Sassy was being held. And he had barely escaped a death trap. They said that God wouldn't place a burden on you if it was more than you could bare. But damn, how heavy did the burden have to be for you to be granted some type of relief?

Did that really matter now? No.

His life was deteriorating, leaving a body with a diabolical brain to maneuver, thereby creating more havoc and chaos for all who were responsible — and those who weren't.

There wasn't much difference between the two at this point in time. Every person, child, whoever he felt like, would pay for his loss — for his pain, misery, suffering, and all thee above.

Weeks ago, he'd been happy, loved by the one who he loved the most. So, why should he allow anyone else to enjoy the pleasures of the world if he couldn't? If he wasn't allowed to live? If he couldn't feel the blissfulness of being with his heart? If he couldn't raise his unborn and bring him up in a way of life he never knew — never had? A life with a father.

All of his dreams were taken —_stolen — away from him. Every fucking bit of them and he knew he wouldn't be able to get any of them back. None of them. No matter how much his soul cried and begged for them. And because of that, he'd paint the city red.

Black was at the top of the list. Right under Stacey and her *people*, whoever they were. He knew they'd be more than hard to find, especially if they were the police. But why pick and choose when they all were a part of the domestic army? Anyone of them would do. Every one of them became the kidnappers in his eyes.

Taking the gun into his hand, he ran his eyes over its nickel-plated surface, admiring its unique form and the power it possessed — the power of causing death. It definitely had more lives to claim by way of the personal justice he planned on issuing.

The phone began to vibrate in his pocket. He'd been expecting this call since the last one. Ace rubbed his thumb over the call icon and listened to Sassy's captors.

The voice offered a light chuckle. "I see you finally understand the consequences of your actions — your mistakes. I bet you've learned to be a good *little* boy now. Huh, Ace?"

Ace remained silent. He gritted his teeth. How funny would shit be once he planted a few bullets in the guy's head with hopefully the same exact grin on the front of his face?

"Now that we see — somewhat —_eye to eye..." He paused briefly. "I want you to bring my fucking shit to the address I'm about to text you. I want all of it… and you. Nobody else. Bring along any of your little friends — or be late — your precious *baby mama* is going to become one with the gawd damn Earth, okay? Oh," he had obviously forgotten something, "and don't bother calling the police…" He giggled, angering Ace even more. "I think she already told you why."

The call went dead, but Ace's demeanor didn't change in the least. He felt it necessary to keep his deadly calm in place because moving or becoming a little bit too emotionally involved could cause his actions to be illogical — something he couldn't afford with their lives on the line.

Whiteboy stepped into the living room, rubbing the drowsiness from his eyes. "What's up?" he asked curiously.

Ace continued to study the gun in awe. "They bout to text an address."

"Who?"

Ace's eyes quickly darted toward him like that was a stupid question.

Whiteboy understood within that same instance. "When? What they talking bout?" He sat on the arm of the couch, wanting to know badly.

"Me, by myself — with *all* the work."

Whiteboy shook his head. "Nah, fuck all that. I'm riding."

Ace knew he'd say that and wouldn't have it any other way. Being honest, he couldn't afford to let it go any other way. He just needed to figure out how to make it work without them knowing.

He didn't want to chance Sassy's safety — if she was still alive. But at the same time, he really needed some back up in case they decided to kill them both. Which smelled more like the situation.

However, he'd sacrifice himself before it got to that point. Beginning to map out his plan, he closed his eyes, titling his head backwards.

Then the phone vibrated yet again. His eyes quickly fixed on the screen. The text had come through.

After scanning the details once, he went to his call log, finding the number and making the call.

. . .

*M*AN, *WHERE THE FUCK THIS NIGGA AT?* B*LACK* ASKED HIMSELF, wondering where the fuck Pee Pee was. The last time he'd talked to him had been the night before. He hadn't heard from him since. It wasn't like him to not at least check in. This was a first.

But then again, he began to remember that he'd told him he was going over to the bitch, Tasha's house. It wasn't a bad option, though at any minute now, they'd have to move to get Black's shit.

Black called him again. Still got the voicemail.

"This stupid ass nigga, man," he said lowly, ready to send some-body to snatch his ass up. There was no pussy that good, especially not when on his watch.

His phone blared to life. Swift sprang to the forefront of his mind as he stared a brief moment at the out-of-town number.

He answered. "Yeah…"

"Mr. Black, how are you feeling this lovely morning?"

"Fucked. I still don't have my muthafucking birds. So, you take a wild guess at how I'm doing." Black wanted to see where he would take this now. He had been playing his little role well, but obviously, Swift forgot that every film had its blind spots.

"Hold your horses. That's what I'm calling you about now. Geez, I got good fucking news. And a bit of bad news." He paused. "Now, which one you want to hear first?" Swift sounded a little too elated.

"Man, just spill the shit," Black ordered, ready to cut through the bullshit and his throat.

"Well, take all the damn fun out of it then, why don'tcha?"

"Ain't nothing fun about my shit missing."

"Okay, okay… Well, your *shit* is on its way here…"

"Where?" Black quickly questioned.

"I'm about to text you the address, and you can deal with the little fuck who's going to bring it."

Black couldn't hold back the grin which crept onto his face. He was already more than aware of who exactly that was. "Aight. Me and my people on the way so text it. Oh, and the bad news?" Black said, gesturing at his two soldiers. He covered the microphone part of his phone, mouthing to them, "Load up."

"You said what?" He wasn't sure he heard him correctly.

"Your buddy, Mr. Diaz, a.k.a. *Pee Pee*, they found him last night with a couple of holes in 'em. You pretty much can guess the rest."

How the fuck did he get caught like that? Black thought, running over the last time he'd seen and talked to him.

"Fuck!" he growled, finding it hard to keep his composure. "Do they have an idea about who did it?"

"No…" Swift returned flatly, figuring it better to leave out the rest of the story. "But it's said that his Challenger was found at a Texaco gas station on Flat Shoals. Right up the street a little bit from where your complex is."

What the fuck is going on? Black wanted badly to know.

"Witnesses say that some — well, one individual was shooting and chased him across the four-way intersection and onto Phillips 66 property. This is where the *guy* tackled 'em then tossed him into a SUV in front of everyone there. Now are you ready for the craziest part of it all?"

Black was listening tentatively. "What?"

"The witnesses are saying that a *white dude* with a hat on did it. Now have y'all been fucking over any hippies lately?" Swift chuckled.

"Text the address," was all Black uttered before he took the initiative in ending the phone call.

The news of Pee Pee getting snatched and flatlined left Black confused. Who would have the balls to pull that off the way Swift had described it? Then, on top of that, a *white dude?*

It wasn't making sense. Black knew of no beefs Pee Pee had — if that had been the reason. And definitely not with any white people.

Nah, it had to be something plotted, seeing as how Pee Pee's whip was found right up the fucking street from his East Hampton spot. *Someone had laid on him*, Black thought. He'd been in the streets for far too long to just accept it as a mere coincidence.

Niggas had waited until he was up the street, away from the team, to try something. And apparently, Pee Pee had caught it and made a break for it and then got chased down and snatched. The person who did it quite obviously had him in mind as the set target.

For what though? Black needed the answer to the question.

A few people came to mind, yet none of them were white or would benefit from it. *But what about Swift?*

He mused over the thought. Of course Swift could have had one of his cronies do it. *Why though?* What could be gained from it? Nothing as far as Black could see. He'd already plotted and *had* stolen too much work from right under his damn nose. And if it hadn't been for them kidnapping Sas…

Ace was suddenly within the center of his mind's eye. Yes, there existed a beef between them, but Ace was in a vulnerable position right now and needed him badly at this point. Black couldn't conjure any logical reason he'd chance getting the bitch back. That wouldn't be helpful or smart on his part.

Finally, Black stood and began to pace back-and-forth while letting his mental slip further into the realm of thoughts. The white dude shit began to form — for some odd reason — with the vivid presence of his old apprentice.

Black shook his head slowly from side to side. A memory came into focus. It was the nigga who Ace had brought to the spot. He was damn near white, almost a little too white to be a nigga.

It had been a minute, so it would be impossible for him to remember the stranger's name. However, the feeling of him actually being the one responsible became more convincing by the second.

Certainly, the nigga knew of the apartment in East Hampton. And on his only and last visit, Pee Pee had aimed an AK at his face. The nigga had singlehandedly knocked out one of his soldiers and had D on his knees with a gun in his mouth.

The guy was reckless with his tongue and was hot headed. So, he could possibly be the one, especially after witnessing firsthand the stress his main man was under.

He'd most definitely make targets out of muthafuckas — on the strength — just to make examples.

He the muthafucking white dude… Black concluded. It made

perfect sense, along with the fact that he'd tell Ace. His loyalty was a little too strong for him not to.

Black was grateful of the third eye he had for this shit. Now that he'd put it together, he summarized that once Ace got his bitch back, he would do away with anybody he felt had their hand in it. Exactly how he — himself — had taught him.

Man, that shit is what it is... You know what the fuck going on. He thought about what Ace said, clearly getting the picture now. Even in his current situation, he had no intention of letting the beef slide until the shit was handled. Black guessed he wanted to let him know that war remained on his mind. Didn't matter if it wasn't at the forefront or not.

Black wouldn't be played so easily though. He now had a way to get his dope back. And once it landed back within the palms of his hands, he'd dead Swift for playing on his intellect while at the same time giving Ace what was due.

"How the fuck niggas think that they can outsmart the brain?" Black said, rubbing his chin.

He would solve it once and for all, leaving him to be the last one standing. He began to think as his phone came to life again.

"I was just thinking about you..."

CHAPTER THIRTEEN

THE TRADE

Speeding close to eighty miles per hour on the expressway, Ace headed toward the address *the people* had sent to him.

Before he took off, he'd met with the team and specifically gave Whiteboy instructions on what to do when he got to the place. Prior to meeting them, him and Black had a face-to-face, which was hard for both of them.

They went over the *woulds* and *coulds* and what needed to happen once they got what they wanted. Then they'd go their separate ways.

The entire time of their little encounter, Ace found it hard not to send a few hot slugs into his head and everybody with him. Sassy's life laid on the line. He'd have to be patient and remind himself of that every minute. But once she was safe…

Ace found it funny that Black hadn't mentioned anything about his missing comrade. He wanted to laugh while he rubbed it in his face yet thought better of it. Again, Sassy was on the line. Knowing Black, he probably didn't give a fuck or didn't know — like he didn't know Ace's true intentions. Which, most likely, were the same as his own.

He cared less about any of it though. If it came down to that while in the process of getting back his love, he would be determined to beat him to the punch. Ace refused to let him — or anybody — get in the way of removing her out of harm's way. Even if she was the only one to make it out, he'd sacrifice himself to see her walk out untouched.

Ace wasn't stupid. He smelled a trap, but if they didn't know that there existed traps both ways, then they were in for a surprise.

Grabbing his cell from the passenger seat, he tapped the power button. The time read 8:45 p.m., leaving him with fifteen more minutes before he'd arrive at the designated location.

Fifteen more minutes for all to be revealed. He was more than ready for it. This shit had eaten him up, devouring the person he knew as himself. Leading him — rather driving him — to the point of no return.

A few days ago, he'd transformed into something other than *Ace* — something not of choice but of necessity. It was a thing only hell was capable of creating. And nothing would stop him from exercising all demons from this moment on.

Slowing the speed of the vehicle down, he drove up the off ramp, bringing it to a stop at the red light. How very dark and gloomy Gwinnett County seemed at the moment. Ace glanced at the route the GPS had set out for him.

"You are one mile and a half from your destination," the computerized voice told him.

Ace pulled the Ruger from under his lap, snatching back the slide. After tucking the pistol down into his waist band, he stepped on the accelerator upon seeing the light flick to green.

In a few more minutes — six according to the GPS — he would be entering a life changing event.

Making a right into the cul-de-sac, he gazed down the murky street then back at the screen of the GPS. Ace wanted to know exactly which house he'd be visiting — the one which would host the mayhem party that was bound to jump off.

He looked over the row of houses which aligned the street on both sides. Immediately, he noticed *the one* which sat away from the street.

Actually, it sat a little farther than any of them. It was the odd one and most definitely would be after tonight.

Switching off the vehicle's lights, he pulled over to the curb, parking in front of the dreary residence. Next, he texted the number he'd been instructed to once he got there. Ace was three minutes early.

Waiting, he began to ponder the possibility of Sassy being tied up somewhere within the insides of the house.

He shook his head. He didn't want to think about the detriment she was suffering. He needed to focus on relieving her of the torment.

Ace looked at the number he was told to text again. He wondered if they might try to play it like he had — renege on the agreement, take the work, then kill him before he had a chance of even seeing her.

However, he wouldn't give up a damn thing until he saw her. Until she was safely by his side. Only then he'd hand over the work, leaving them to be dealt with by Black.

Adjusting the straps on his waist, Ace quickly pretended to be straightening out his Foreign Republic t-shirt. The shadowy figure had come into sight, moving directly in his direction.

Ace studied the darkened figure, now noticing the semi-automatic weapon he toted, as if he was one of those special ops dudes. He wore all-black with a ski mask over his face. This was a good sign to Ace. The only time people didn't want you to see their faces was when you'd be able to describe them later. And later meant living.

Coming to the driver's door, the man signaled for him to get out.

Without hesitating, Ace opened the car door, expecting some form of procedural pat down. But there was none, not even a word. The masked man pointed the muzzle of his weapon toward the house.

Another good sign, Ace thought as he proceeded up the driveway with the individual a foot or two behind. It felt like the figure imitated every single step he had made because he heard nothing besides his own feet hitting the concrete.

Ace smirked in the darkness, continuing to move. These people were unaware of the character they were dealing with. And he would use this to his advantage.

Getting closer to the house, Ace was about to turn in the direction of the porch. Quickly, the muzzle of the gun objected, pressing against the side of his arm, steering him to keep straight. They were heading for the back of the house.

Barely able to see in the pitch-black darkness, Ace walked the length of the pavement until the under footing became dirt. After a few more steps, he noticed a light which came from the inside of a doorway.

Without having to be steered, Ace treaded toward the threshold, stepping into the light. He had stepped into a kitchen.

He glanced around and got the impression that some junkies had to be the previous squatters of the place, nasty — very nasty — junkies. The stove and countertops were full of all sorts of trash, molded food, and things which had no place in a home period.

The sink was filled with a green liquid similar to sewage with a few mildewed dishes poking out. Then, there was the floor. Certain parts had been ripped out for only God knew why.

Damn, I hope they didn't keep her in this mut hole the entire time, Ace said to himself, wishing at this moment that they would have to bring her here. This shit had been the most disgusting shit he'd ever seen.

He stopped after making it to the hallway. Ace waited for the individual to guide him in the right direction, seeing as how he could go either right or left. He got an answer. The muzzle touched his right arm again slightly, pushing him toward the left.

This was for sure a jay's haven. He walked over the rubbish in the hallway then into the living room. Instantly, he noticed the black coverings over the front windows. Now it became obvious that they really didn't want anyone to know they were here.

The black drapes had done a great job too. The light in the living room was extra bright, probably the brightest part of the house. Yet you'd never be able to tell it if you looked at the house from the street. Even if you stood on the front porch, you still wouldn't see this illumination. Hell, he hadn't, and he was just out in front, looking for some indication that someone other than him and the masked individual was present.

Poking Ace in the back, the masked person ushered him over toward a corner in the room. He kept his gaze on the man as he backpedaled with the weapon aimed mid-level. His eyes were locked on Ace's as though he was trying to read his thoughts.

Only if you could, Ace thought before finally asking, "Where is she?" He got no response. A few minutes passed in silence, which Ace grew tired of real quick. He hadn't come here to sit and stare. But at the same time, he understood that he'd have to be patient if he wanted her back —_alive.

The individual continued to stare, like he was a fucking statue. It amazed Ace that a person could be so disciplined to keep his posture without wavering even a little bit.

Ace wanted to say something to at least irritate the fucking mute though decided against it. He began to hear the sounds of footsteps coming from the hallway.

It was time.

A middle-aged, white dude appeared from beyond the threshold. He didn't have on a mask or the dark attire his accomplice preferred. He matched the description of a college professor more than that of someone involved in dope and the kidnapping of a pregnant woman. However, he did look exactly like what Sassy had told him. The police.

His icy blue eyes set on Ace as a big grin spread across his face. The man walked over to the wooden table which sat opposite of Ace. Sliding his hand over the surface, he removed a good amount of dust then took a seat.

"Good evening, Mr. Jackson —_or would you prefer being called *Ace*?" Ace recognized the voice as the same one from the calls.

This guy was definitely the police because he'd spoken his real name, which nobody ever used. Hell, he had even forgotten it at times.

Ace twisted his lips. He'd been played from the beginning. If this dude was the police, then Stacey was too. *Fuck!* She'd played him right into this predicament when he should've known that all the college shit she displayed was an act — an act executed to the tee.

The guy chuckled. "Okay, straight to the business then, shall we?

So, where the fuck is the dope?" His demeanor had changed within an instance to one other than the muthafucka who'd first walked in.

This, Ace knew, was the real him. "Where is Sassy?"

"She's around," he calmly returned, smiling at his partner as if he found the question amusing.

"Well, it a be here when she is," Ace told him, not really interested in playing the little game the man obviously intended on playing.

"Oh, it's not with you? Well, Mr. Jackson, that's a very bad thing…"

Ace cut him off. "Nigga, either you bring her here or *we* both suffer the consequences — together," he said matter-of-factly. Ace chose his words wisely, knowing the officer would catch his drift.

He wanted to smirk after seeing how his statement caused both of them to kill their giggling.

The man stared him down a moment, like he was weighing the chances of Ace being serious or bluffing.

Ace was experienced at tricking people with his facial expressions. It was an art he'd used many times in the streets, and doing so to this clown would be nothing.

The guy smiled again. "I don't think that you are *that* stupid, Mr. Jackson."

"Then the joke will be on you."

The man glanced down at his hands, rubbing them as if he saw something on them. Ace took it as his way of nervously fidgeting. "You play a dangerous game, Mr. Jackson…"

"I don't play games. I do believe in insurance though."

"I can agree with that. So, we'll handle this as soon as…" His words trailed off. His phone blared to life.

"Yeah…" he answered. "Great. Okay, just come on round the back," he finished, ending the phone call.

Ace hoped the call was in relation to Sassy because there wasn't shit else to talk about. He watched him remove a nine-millimeter Beretta from within his suit jacket and aim it at him.

The guy kept his eyes on Ace as he told his comrade, "Go get the bitch."

Ace listened for anything that would give him a hint as to whether she'd been outside or somewhere within this house. If it was the latter, then he knew more of the man's company was on the way — and for unknown reasons.

And the latter it was.

She was here the whole time, he thought after hearing the latch of a door click somewhere off down the hallway. Ace wondered if she'd heard him and knew that he was here to get her away from all this madness.

Footsteps began to resonate through the thin walls of the interior, coming toward where they were. His heart started to pound harder with anticipation as the steps got closer and closer. He was ready to be reunited with his love, his girl — his life.

Ace wanted to smile but couldn't. Maybe once this came to an end. Not right now though. This shit was far from over with.

Then, a person came into the living room.

Ace stared in disbelief at the unexpected individual who'd just made a surprising appearance. *What the fuck?* He became confused to the point of stiffness. His nemesis, Black, smiled broadly as if he'd read his mind.

Of course him and Black had put a hell of a scheme together to fuck over whoever these muthafuckas were, but this hadn't been a part of the plan.

"Ace, what up?" Black flashed all thirty-two golds. He knew he would catch him off guard with this shocking revelation. Maybe now Ace would see that no matter what he thought or did, Black was always a few steps ahead. That was what made him the king of this street shit.

Ace's throat went dry. It became hard for him to swallow or say anything. Here stood the nigga he hated the most, on the same side as the people who were responsible for his very own shit being taken. It wasn't making sense. These people had plotted and used Ace as a pawn to execute the transgression on his former leader. Yet now, both parties — from his point of view — seemed to have been on the same side this entire time. But if they were on the same team, why play the double cross games?

It was not adding up, period. Ace understood Black all too well. Never had he been the type to put his shit on the line by having niggas play with it and definitely not to reel a nigga in just to get some revenge. He wouldn't waste time on chancing his own money. Yeah, probably somebody else's, but not his.

Right now though, Ace knew he didn't possess enough time to piece the puzzle together. Maybe later he could, if such a time came, which seemed slim to none at this very moment.

Things were about to get real bloody.

"Well, well, ain't this an unusual reunion?" chuckled the cop with a clap of his hands.

Ace remained silent, contemplating the chances of him getting Sassy out alive. Black's sudden appearance had sealed his fate. And had Whiteboy not accompanied him on this rescue mission, he might have become even more discouraged by the fact that he'd be the only one to leave the earth tonight. He didn't care as long as she got out.

With that, a smile came to his face. Everything he had in his body would be used to make sure *they* all went to hell as one big fucking *party*.

Just her, he repeated to himself like a chant. At this moment, all he wanted was to see her one last time before he sacrificed his life for hers. That was the only thing Ace needed.

"Nah, I'd say this is more like a going away party," Black let out, loving the way he'd outsmarted his little defector.

Ace nodded his head, silently agreeing with him on that note. He wanted badly to let him know how truthful his words were before he pulled the Ruger .45 and blasted away. Again, he needed to see her first.

Then, within a split second, she emerged from the hallway — dirty, beaten… broken yet still as beautiful as ever. She was still perfect in his eyes.

Ace stared at her, and she stared back. Her expression changed with every passing second through a multitude of mixed emotions. He could tell she wanted to break down right here and now. But he didn't want her to. This wasn't over. Hell, he wanted to smile, hug, and kiss her before he told her how much he loved her. Though he couldn't because this wasn't over with. Only God could allow him the chance to do such before whatever would happen.

"Go on to your superman…" the cop told her, signaling with his pistol.

Quickly, Sassy stepped over the wooden floor, tears spewing out the web of her eyes joyfully.

Ace took in her delicate physique, angered by what he saw. Yet, at the same time, he was grateful to have her so close to him. It had been way too long. Ace touched her but only to guide her behind his protective body. It was impossible for either of them to give closure to one another under their current situation.

"Now, the dope?" the cop insisted, aiming the gun at Ace's forehead.

Ace was about to tell him. But he knew — like Black did — where the bricks were. He hated Black now more than ever. Stupidly, he had previously informed him on the exact location. Bad move number two, he realized.

Black smiled at Ace's expression. "I know where they are…"

Confused, the cop glanced over at him. "You know where the dope is?"

"Yep…" Swiftly, Black removed the gun from his waistline. "And you know what…" he paused, placing his marker on Ace, causing a shriek to escape Sassy's lips.

"What's that?" The guy raised an arched eyebrow.

"I know exactly how it got there…"

Instantly, the cop's look shifted from sugar to shit as he watched Black, within the blink of an eye, sweep the gun toward his skull and fire.

The man looked as if he was about to say something when the bullet entered his face, taking a chunk of brain matter as it exited his head. Another one followed the first instantaneously.

A scream left Sassy. Ace quickly drew the Ruger, seeing the perfect opportunity to flatline Black, who turned a little too fast toward him with his aim set.

Ace squeezed. Nothing. He squeezed twice more and got the same result as the first time. Ace stared at the weapon, bewildered. *What the fuck is wrong with it?*

His eyes went back to Black, defeated. He was like a deer in front of headlights.

"You should of picked better niggas to fuck wit…" was all he heard before seeing the sparks flash, sending him into an abode of blackness.

"In breaking news… Last night at ten forty p.m., Gwinnett County police responded to McDaniel Street, where four people were found dead. Surprisingly, one of them were undercover D.E.A. agent from the Atlanta division.

"No identities have been disclosed as of this moment.

"Among the victims laid a pregnant female, who police are trying to identify, along with another female and one other male.

"A fifth victim, who police say survived the massacre, has been placed in the intensive care unit at Grady Memorial Hospital.

"Detectives say they have no leads in the case right now but suspect that it involved narcotics after discovering an undisclosed amount of narcotics outside of the residence."

To Be Continued

IN The Streetz 3
Coming Soon!

REVIEW

Did you enjoy the read?
Let us know how much by leaving us a review on Amazon and
Goodreads.

OTHER BOOKS BY

Santa Sent Me A Real One For Christmas

Wet Dreams on Lockdown: The Unit Manager

Thug Me The Right Way 2

Thug Me The Right Way 3

Seizing A Gangsta's Heart For The Summer

By **Nai**

A Setup For Revenge

A Setup For Revenge 2

Wet Dreams On Lockdown: The Librarian

By **Ashley Williams**

Ridin' For You

Ridin' For You, Too

Trickin' on a Heaux for Christmas: A BBW Love Story

Homie Hoppin' For The Holidays

Wet Dreams on Lockdown: The Female C.O

Letters Of His Love

By **Telia Teanna**

The State's Witness

The State's Witness 2

The State's Witness 3

This Time Won't You Save Me

This Time Won't You Save Me 2

His Summer Side Piece

By **Kyiris Ashley**

Stuck In The Trenches

Stuck In The Trenches 2

By **Huff Tha Great**

The Swipe

The Swipe 2

By **Toōla**

Melted the Heart of a Menace

Wet Dreams On Lockdown: Lieutenant Grace

By P. Wise

Merry Trapmas: Ice & Frost

By **Mia Sky**

Thug Me The Right Way

By **DiamondATL & Nai**

Atlantastan

Atlantastan 2

By **Chris Green**

IN The Streetz

By **Tron Hill**

Wet Dreams on Lockdown: The Male C.O

By **Tamyra Griffin**

Wet Dreams On Lockdown: The Counselor

By **Paris Iman**

Wet Dreams On Lockdown: The Warden

By **Shawnice**

Wet Dreams On Lockdown: The Captain

By **TN Jones**

**Coming Soon From
<u>URBAN AINT DEAD</u>**

The Hottest Summer Ever 2
THE G-CODE
Tales 4rm Da Dale 2
How To Invest In The Stock Market From Prison
By **Elijah R. Freeman**

Hittaz 5
Coldhearted 3
By **Lou Garden Price, Sr.**

Good Girl Gone Rogue 3
By **Manny Black**

Despite The Odds 2
Hittin' Licks For The Holidays: Chicago
By **Juhnell Morgan**

The Swipe 3
By **Toōla**

Charge It To The Game 3
By **Nai**

This Time Won't You Save Me 3
By **Kyiris Ashley**

Ridin' Forever
By **Telia Teanna**

Atlantastan 3
By **Chris Green**

BOOKS BY

URBAN AINT DEAD's C.E.O

<u>Elijah R. Freeman</u>

Triggadale

Triggadale 2

Triggadale 3

Tales 4rm Da Dale

The Hottest Summer Ever

Murda Was The Case

Murda Was The Case 2

Murda Was The Case 3

Hittin' Licks For The Holidays: Atlanta

Wet Dreams On Lockdown: The Nurse

How To Publish A Book From Prison